"There's no shame in hard work. Try it!"

Chantal's words made no impression on the marquis. "Why are you angry?" he asked. He seemed determined to act the benevolent *patron*.

"Why?" she choked. "You curtail our local supplies of material, you command the villagers not to work for us, then you laugh at us!"

His voice was smooth. "I'm sorry you found my amusement hurtful. *Ma belle châtaigne*," he breathed, gently kissing her lashes. "I'm enchanted—are you ice or fire?"

"I read somewhere that you Frenchmen have an unlimited capacity for gallantry," she snapped. "But why bother to waste compliments on a drudge?"

His jaw tightened, yet his tone remained mild. "Can't you recognize good old-fashioned courtship, *chérie*?"

Suddenly tears flooded her eyes. The quivering she dreaded erupted inside her—a deep yearning to respond.

Other titles by
MARGARET ROME
IN HARLEQUIN ROMANCES

Other titles by
MARGARET ROME
IN HARLEQUIN PRESENTS

Many of these titles are available at your local bookseller.

For a free catalogue listing all available Harlequin Romances,
send your name and address to:

HARLEQUIN READER SERVICE,
M.P.O. Box 707, Niagara Falls, N.Y. 14302
Canadian address: Stratford, Ontario, Canada N5A 6W2

Champagne Spring

by

MARGARET ROME

Harlequin Books

TORONTO·LONDON·NEW YORK·AMSTERDAM
SYDNEY·HAMBURG·PARIS·STOCKHOLM

Original hardcover edition published in 1979
by Mills & Boon Limited

ISBN 0-373-02332-4

Harlequin edition published May 1980

CHAPTER ONE

'Er ... Peter?' Chantal braced herself before voicing the tentative suggestion. 'Would you like to tidy up a little before Uncle James arrives?' The scowl she dreaded darkened her brother's features. 'If you'd just change your shirt and run a comb through your hair,' she continued doggedly.

'Oh, for heaven's sake!' Irritably, he swung his legs from the arm of his chair and stood up to glare across the width of the tiny sitting-room. 'Nag, nag, nag, all you ever do is nag!'

She drew in an exasperated breath, determined not to be cowed by her young brother's arrogance. 'Peter, must you be so childish? Such an attitude contradicts all your arguments. Your seventeenth birthday is behind you, on your own insistence you're no longer a schoolboy. In a short while,' surreptitiously she crossed her fingers for luck, 'you'll find a job, and as childish tantrums are hardly likely to find favour in a business establishment don't you think it's about time you began acting more responsibly? Office juniors are expected to be polite, helpful, and to fit unobtrusively into the pattern of their surroundings.'

'All of which,' he retorted bitterly, 'judging from my observations during the few short interviews I've been unfortunate enough to attend, seem to consist entirely of mud-brown walls and slush-grey

5

floor coverings. My future is a canvas,' he waxed dramatic, 'pure white and undefiled, and you, Sis, wield the artist's brush! What right have *you* to decide that my canvas should be daubed grey and brown?'

They glared at each other, the gangling schoolboy-cum-youth standing tall as his sister, with wrists protruding beneath the cuffs of a navy-blue blazer that had only just managed to see him through his final term, as had regulation grey trousers that had become so weak at the seams Chantal had to spend half an hour each evening mending slits that appeared with monotonous regularity in the thread-bare material.

She winced from the fierce blaze of animosity emanating from his direction, but determined, just this once, not to be browbeaten, she tossed her head and stepped forward into the path of sunshine piercing through windowpanes, unaware that her coil of glorious hair glowed rich dark red before she moved into shadow, when it adopted the depth and texture of chestnut-coloured velvet.

'Necessity, together with your own pigheaded stubbornness, decreed the direction that your future is to take, my lad, not I!' She spoke tersely in order to discourage a choking sob which, had it been heard, would have shattered the aplomb that was her main ally in her fight to control her wayward brother. 'If you'd listen to me, you'd go on with your studies in the hope of getting a university place.'

'*No way!*' he interrupted hotly. 'I mean to start earning.'

'So be it,' she snapped, suffering the sinking sensation that had terminated each phase of the interminable argument. 'I can't force you against your will to go on with your schooling, but I can and do insist that you embark upon the sort of career that would have met with Father's approval.'

'But I don't want——'

'Just look at the time!' A quick glance at her watch confirmed that their visitor's arrival was imminent. 'Just this once will you please do as I ask—you know how untidiness offends Uncle James.'

'Oh, very well!' he exploded. 'If it will keep you quiet. Though why I should have to dress up simply because the family solicitor is paying us a visit I simply don't know!'

'He was Father's oldest and dearest friend,' she reminded him quietly. 'Have you forgotten how kind he was to us when we were children and how helpful he's been since Father's death? I sometimes wonder,' she paused to steady a tremble in her voice, 'how we would have fared without him.'

Peter was young enough to suffer a shamefaced blush. 'I wonder what it is he wants to discuss with us,' he queried gruffly and for the umpteenth time since the solicitor's letter had arrived a couple of days previously.

'I've no idea.' Patiently, Chantal returned the stock reply, gritting her teeth against an impulse to chide him for shuffling his feet. She was weary of his accusations that she was forever 'getting at him' and not a little hurt by them. Latterly, they had been living in a constant state of friction and according to Peter it was all her fault—she nagged, she pressured, she was forever critical. Inwardly she knew that the accusation was undeserved, yet nevertheless she felt guilty. Once, not so long ago, they had laughed, joked, and exchanged fond hugs almost every day. All that had changed when seemingly overnight her cheerful, loving young brother had developed moods of deep introspection, had begun to tilt against even her mild authority by deliberately adopting opposing viewpoints, by being argumentative, and by putting off any job he was asked to do until the last possible moment—sometimes ignoring her requests completely. All in all, he had managed to make life pretty intolerable, only the occasional days of normality that seemed like flashbacks to a former existence serving to make the situation bearable.

'Perhaps it's a windfall!' His moody features lightened with a look of optimism. 'A source of income that was overlooked when Uncle James was settling Father's affairs.'

'All that Father possessed was the few hundred pounds he'd saved and the pension that terminated at his death,' Chantal reminded him gently, saddened by the memory of their recent loss yet finding comfort in the fact that Peter had at last found it possible to speak of the father whose sudden death two months earlier had left him distraught, bewildered and completely lacking in motivation.

He had put forward very negative views: he would *not* finish his schooling, he would *not* try for a place at university, he would *not* be a burden upon his sister, but whenever the subject of a career had been broached his replies had always been vague, evasive.

'I could ask Uncle James if there's likely to be an opening in his firm,' she continued her train of thought aloud. 'He keeps insisting that if ever we're in need of help we're to get in touch with him immediately.'

'Mud and slush!' Peter vented his resentment upon the lino surrounding the carpet, scoring so deeply with a rubber heel it squealed a piercing protest.

Resisting an impulse to scream, Chantal schooled her voice to calmness. 'Jobs are not easy to come by, especially when you have no qualifications. I think you ought to be grateful for any chance——'

'To be pushed around?' he objected rudely. 'To be forced to work in an office when it's the very last place I'd choose? Unlike you, Sis, I do not rush around thanking everyone for nothing or apologising when I've done nothing wrong. You're always at it, showing gratitude for the very air you breathe, saying you're sorry when someone steps on *your* toes. Why don't you cultivate more self-assurance? If you insist upon acting like a doormat you'll surely be stood upon!'

When he rushed out of the room she sank into a chair feeling she had battled her way through a storm. Wearily, she considered his accusation and was bound to admit that perhaps he had a point; she *was* too meek, too eager to comply with the wishes of others. In common with her late father, all she asked of life was peace and happiness, yet it was becoming obvious that if she were to survive her brother's angry adolescence her outlook would have

to change. He had scoffed at her for being a doormat, conveniently overlooking the fact that he was
the one who made the most use of her services. A
gentle wiping of feet she did not mind—unfortunately, the faster Peter grew the more she seemed
in danger of being trampled!

When, a quarter of an hour later, she answered
the doorbell her expression was composed, showing
no hint of strain to the man whom she greeted with
a fond kiss.

'How nice of you to visit us, Uncle James.'

The elderly solicitor returned her kiss. 'A combined duty and business visit, I'm ashamed to say,
my dear. I had imagined that semi-retirement would
allow me more time to spend with you and Peter
but, alas, the opposite is the case. I worry about you
both,' he frowned, handing over his hat and coat.

'There's no need, Uncle,' she reprimanded, pre-
ceding him along the narrow hallway, 'we're perfectly capable of looking after our own affairs, you
must concentrate all your attention upon your in-
valid wife.'

'Considerate as ever, my dear,' he approved, accepting her invitation to sit in one of the shabby old
armchairs positioned either side of the fireplace.
Sinking down, he seemed to luxuriate in long-
forgotten comfort. 'How I abominate those new-
fangled armchairs that are all buttons, leather, and
hard upholstery! As I often used to remark to your
father——' He paused his eyes falling upon the
chair opposite, its emptiness underlining their loss.

Swallowing a lump in her throat, Chantal offered,
'You'll take a cup of tea? Everything is ready, just

the kettle to boil. I'll go and see to it.'

When she returned with a loaded tea-tray Peter, with slicked-back hair, wearing a clean shirt and—wonder of wonders—a tie, was dutifully exchanging small talk with their guest.

Beaming at her across the tea-tray, her uncle asked a trifle apologetically, 'I hope you found no difficulty in getting time off for this meeting? Unfortunately, my time is so committed I could not manage any other day. One of my partners could have attended to the business in hand, of course, but as I've always had a special interest in you both I preferred to see to it myself.'

Aching with curiosity, but aware that he would not be rushed into an explanation until he was ready, Chantal shrugged. 'No problem. It's half-term, the school is closed until Tuesday.'

He continued observing the pleasantries, enquiring after their health and future plans but in a manner so abstracted it was easy to guess that a subject of greater importance was uppermost in his mind. The tea-cups had been filled and emptied several times when eventually he surprised them with the question:

'How much do you know about your late mother's family?'

'Very little.' Chantal's eyes reflected puzzlement.

'Nothing whatsoever!' Peter added simultaneously.

'Father seemed to find it difficult to talk to us about Mother,' Chantal continued slowly, dredging her mind in an effort to recall the very few facts she had gleaned about the mother who had died giving birth to Peter. 'I vaguely recollect his mentioning that she was of French origin, but as no letters or visits were ever exchanged I assumed that she had no living relatives.'

'And as Father had none either, we've become pretty well accustomed to regarding ourselves as penniless orphans,' Peter offered, his cheerful grin robbing his words of the least hint of self-pity.

'Strange ...' Uncle James looked taken aback, then with a sigh of resignation conceded, 'But there again, it's perhaps a mistake to prolong family connections unduly, to insist that people, however much antipathy they feel towards one another, should pretend affection when no affection exists.'

'Who are you talking about, Uncle James?' Chantal was perplexed, unable to follow his train of thought.

'Your relatives, my dear,' he explained dryly, 'and your grandmother in particular—Hélène, Comtesse d'Estrées—a wonderful old matriarch who insisted upon remaining head of the *Etablissement La Roque à Remi* in spite of her very advanced years.'

'*Our grandmother?* You mean we have a grandmother? I had no idea!'

'Had ...' he corrected, sadly shaking his head. 'She died a month ago. Which is why I'm here today, to discuss the contents of her will.'

Chantal and Peter exchanged incredulous stares. For years they had existed as a tight-knit trio, father, daughter and son, with Chantal playing the role of little mother, subconsciously striving to supply the feminine influence she had always sensed was lacking. Yet throughout those years a grandmother had been lurking in the background, a mature woman of wisdom who could have advised, cosseted, loved—and been loved in return.

'Why ... ?' Chantal breathed aching regret.

With a grumpy cough their solicitor cleared his throat and groped for a handkerchief to wipe over misted spectacles. 'It's a very long story, my dear. I found it impossible not to admire your grandmother, she possessed a business acumen that was the envy of many men. Even if she had not belonged to one of the great champagne families whose daughters, known as the 'Champagne Girls', were the great catches of their time, her personality would have guaranteed her a place in Champenois history. I was privileged to meet her many years ago—it saddens me greatly to learn that you two, her own flesh and blood, were denied that right.'

Peter leant forward, his youthful jawline tense. 'Why did we never meet her, do you know?'

'Your father was always reticent on the subject of his in-laws, but chancing an educated guess, I'd blame family strife—the most bitter strife of all. Outsiders should never attempt to apportion blame, but I must admit that my sympathies have always lain with your father. To help you understand his difficulties,' Uncle James went on, 'I must explain the character of your mother's people, the Champenois—true sons and daughters of the French province, Champagne. Theirs is a paradoxical nature that makes it impossible, unless they themselves should allow it, for an alien to get to know them well. They can don at will an expressionless mask that shows no glimpse of their feelings. They

use reserve as a deterrent, a warning not to en-
croach too far upon friendship. And yet at the
flicker of an eyelash they can erupt into laughter,
finding humour in situations that would arouse
only compassion or pity in others.'

Chantal gave a small start, reminded of a trait in
Peter that she had often found worrying, a lack of
sensitivity that enabled him to find malicious
amusement in the misfortunes of others. Often he
made physical disability the butt of his biting wit,
yet conversely, he possessed a charm so devastating
he managed always to claim the forgiveness of his
victims.

Their solicitor's voice again claimed her attention.

'There was little evidence of this reserve when
your father and I first entered the province of
Champagne as members of the British Army of
Liberation. We were greeted with ecstatic delight,
and as our transport rolled through the countryside everyone seemed determined to shake the hands
of the soldiers who had freed them from German
occupation. Not the least determined was the
woman who was later to become your grandmother
—the Comtesse d'Estrées, who all during the war
had managed to retain control of the great champagne house, La Roque à Remi, and to run it almost single-handed during her husband's absence.

'Even I, a senior army officer, found the adula-
tion heady, so you can imagine the effect it had upon
your father, who was at that time an extremely
young, raw lieutenant, awkward in the role of conquering hero.'

Glancing at Chantal, he smiled wryly, correctly interpreting her puzzled frown. 'You're finding it difficult to picture either myself or your father as a conquering warrior?'

She blushed, wishing her expression would not so clearly mirror her thoughts. 'I'm sorry, the war took place such a long time ago,' she stumbled in her embarrassment, 'you must excuse me if I can't quite imagine my father taking part in what's now classed as history.'

'Your family history,' he reminded, pained by the realisation that to her he must appear a subject of antiquity.

'Do go on!' Peter urged, impatient of the interruption.

Willingly their solicitor obliged. 'Personally, I was not the least bit surprised when the Comtesse's attitude hardened immediately she became aware of the attraction that had sprung up between a penniless young lieutenant and her only daughter. I hesitate to use a cliché, but love at first sight is the only way to describe the impact your parents had upon each other. When their devotion became too obvious to be ignored I tried, as his senior officer, to prepare your father for the opposition I felt certain would come, but he refused to listen, refused to accept that any mortal would be cruel enough to try to separate two people who were so deeply and emotionally committed.'

When he paused for a moment, Chantal admitted, 'I have no memory of my mother, but Father kept a photograph of her in one of his drawers and I often used to steal a peep.'

'I'd love to see it.' The solicitor's head jerked up.

Wishing she had kept her thoughts to herself, she glanced quickly at Peter, then choked the reply. 'I'm sorry, it isn't possible. Father was clutching the photograph when we found him, so ... I asked that it should not be removed.'

Peter jumped up and stalked across to the window. She knew he was fighting back tears when his voice bit harshly across his shoulder. 'If dead ashes must be raked over for heaven's sake let's get on with it!'

A man of less sensitivity might have taken Peter's attitude as an afront to his dignity, but to Chantal's relief their solicitor agreed with him.

'You're quite right, painful matters should be disposed of as speedily as possible. I'll be brief, any minor details can be discussed at a later date.

'Your father's request to the Comtesse to marry her daughter was met with a scandalised refusal. They were both too young, she insisted, the match was entirely unsuitable. Then without warning her daughter was whisked out of his sight—sent to live with relatives, I suspect—and as your father's duties did not allow him time to go in search of her he had no option but to accept the situation.

'Shortly after that our company split up and your father and I lost touch. The war had been over for five years, we were both civilians, when I received a letter asking me to be best man at his wedding. Yes,' he nodded in response to Chantal's gasp of surprise, 'he'd searched until he found his bride. The only drawback was the fact that, so far as the Comtesse was concerned, nothing had changed. She forbade the marriage, so they married against her will. As a consequence, the Comtesse disowned your mother—consequently she must have been unaware that her daughter had died at a tragically early age, leaving her husband to cope alone with a five-year-old daughter and an infant son.'

'Father could have written to her!' Chantal burst out.

'Of course he couldn't!' Peter flung savagely from the window. 'No man with any pride would risk being accused of scrounging, which is what—judging from the little we've learned about our grandmother—she would immediately have assumed.'

'She does appear to have been a proud, unforgiving sort of person,' Chantal agreed, 'and yet,' her green eyes quizzed, 'you mentioned earlier, Uncle James, that you'd come here today to discuss the contents of her will, which leads me to assume that we're to be beneficiaries. Does that prove that she did eventually relent?'

He sighed. 'How I wish I could reply yes to that question, my dear, but unfortunately I can't. You're correct in one respect, Peter and yourself are each to receive a share of your grandmother's estate.'

Peter shot upright, his face alive with excitement. 'My guess was right, Sis, it *is* a windfall!' He shot her a triumphant look.

But Chantal, sensing that a lot remained unexplained, remained calm. 'Such generosity is hardly the act of an unforgiving woman, Uncle James, and yet you say our grandmother's attitude didn't soften?'

'That is correct. Two factors are responsible for

the fact that you and Peter are to inherit part of your grandmother's property. Do either of you have knowledge of the Code Napoléon?'

Eagerly, Peter nodded. 'I learnt about it last term. It's a Code of Law prepared under the direction of Napoleon Bonaparte which forms the substance of the laws of France and Belgium. Equality in the eyes of the law, justice and common sense are its keynotes.'

His uncle nodded approval. 'One clause in the Code concerns inheritance and stipulates that most of a deceased person's property must be divided equally among members of his family. Therefore your grandmother had no say in the matter. Her daughter was bound by law to inherit a share in her estate, a share which, because of her death, is to be passed on to her children. Sadly, however,' he directed Chantal a sorrowful look, 'being fully aware of the circumstances, your grandmother proved that she carried her grievances to the grave by making sure that most of her assets were shared out amongst minor members of her family before she died.

'Which brings me to the second factor involved in your inheritance, but before I elaborate, I must explain that the vineyards in the Champagne district are split into a great number of small plots owned almost exclusively by true Champenois, who guard each square inch of their land with obsessive possessiveness. Champagne firms of world reknown have not been able to persuade small growers to sell their plots. Though they would much prefer to own their own vineyards and work them with salaried workers, they're forced to buy the grapes they need from the Champenois proprietors. This tradition of ownership was behind your grandmother's reluctance to transfer her vineyards to the House. Fortunately for you both, she hung on too long, which is why, as her only remaining blood relatives, each of you now owns three acres of the most valuable Champagne vineyards.'

He sat back, well pleased with the effect his words had had upon his two listeners. They were stunned, each deep in thought, wrestling with disappointment brought about for two different reasons—Peter wondering what could be gained from a parcel of land no bigger than a couple of football pitches; Chantal full of regret at having found a grandmother and losing her again within the space of an hour.

Their solicitor's voice penetrated their absorption, sounding far distant. 'If you're pondering on the best way to cash in on your inheritance, I'm happy to be able to tell you that you have no need to worry, the solution is at hand in the form of a certain Marquis de la Roque who took over from your grandmother as Head of the Establissement la Roque à Remi. For a very satisfactory sum of money indeed, he's prepared to buy you out. Tomorrow he's flying from France in order to visit you personally. On his behalf, I've been requested to present his compliments and to ask if it will be convenient for you to receive him here, in your own home, at approximately two o'clock.'

CHAPTER TWO

AFTER a night of endless discussion Chantal awoke heavy-eyed. Sunshine was flooding into her bedroom, yet she rose with reluctance, feeling a premonition of disaster. Then realising that in a few short hours the Marquis de la Roque was due to arrive, she was galvanised into action.

Would he expect to be served lunch, or could she assume that he would have eaten before he arrived? To offer tea might be better, but then again, perhaps Frenchmen did not indulge in the very English ritual. She would have to extend some sort of hospitality! Inspiration struck. A drink should suffice. Vaguely she recalled hearing mentioned that the French were partial to Pernod, a revolting-sounding drink tasting of aniseed. She would send Peter to the supermarket to buy a bottle—and a bottle of brandy, too, just in case!

To her surprise, Peter nodded instant agreement when she broached the suggestion. He had demolished his breakfast without a word, seemingly deeply involved in his own thoughts. Noting his expression of tense preoccupation, she teased lightly:

'Though our inheritance promises to bring us quite a bit of money, it will hardly be large enough to cause us worry about how to spend it.' She cast a frown around the small kitchen, mentally tabulating in order of importance what needed to be replaced. A new toaster was a must; in parts, the lino was worn almost into holes, and new curtains would immeasurably brighten the house's rather drab exterior. But even those items could wait, *if only*——

'Peter,' she blurted impulsively, 'now that we have prospects of becoming financially secure, won't you reconsider your decision not to continue with your schooling? Scholastic qualifications are bound to improve your prospects, whichever career you eventually decide upon.'

'I have decided.' His quiet statement halted her in mid-breath. 'The job I want to do calls not for diplomas but for a skill that I already possess. I want to grow vines, Sis!' He leant across the table to stress his sincerity. 'I've been reading up on it—I knew I'd seen some reference to the Champagne district, so I rummaged through my books until I'd unearthed the information I wanted, then spent the best part of the night reading about the planting, grafting, cultivating and harvesting of vines. I found the whole subject fascinating. As I read, it was as if a small pinpoint of light appeared on my mind's horizon, then slowly grew until, with blinding insight, I recognised that it was my lodestar, a magnet guiding me towards the knowledge that growing things is what I'm best at, and is what I want to do for the rest of my life. If you care anything at all about my happiness, Sis, you won't try to put obstacles in my path.'

Though he kept his fingers crossed, luck deserted him.

'I've never heard anything so outrageously idiotic!' Chantal exploded. 'You may have the advantage of a little knowledge gleaned from books, but even I, ignorant as I am, realise that vine growing is a complicated procedure and that success in such a specialised field can't be achieved without years of experience and practice.'

Peter jumped to his feet. 'And how do you gain experience, tell me that!' he challenged mutinously. 'If someone shows an aptitude for maths or physics one naturally progresses via college or university until he has a complete grasp of his chosen subject. My aptitude is for growing things—it may have been *inherited*, have you thought of that!' he fiercely stated. 'My university could be Champagne where already I feel I belong, and my tutors the Champenois, men whose expertise is second to none.'

When he had stormed out on his errand to the supermarket, Chantal vented frustration and impotent fear by shaking cushions to the point of threatened disintegration, beating rugs until their tassels frayed and by polishing furniture with such ferocity that by the time Peter returned in a rather subdued mood the house was sparkling as a new pin.

Plonking two bottles swathed in tissue paper on to the nearest table, he strode across to slide an arm around her still trembling shoulders.

'I'm sorry I sprang it on you so suddenly, Sis. Naturally, your first impulse was to regard my idea as the whim of a vacillating adolescent, but I swear to you it's not. Think about it,' he urged, turning on all the charm of which he was capable, 'ask yourself whose produce has, for the past two seasons, gained most awards in the local flower and vegetable show? Who's the young upstart blessed with so-called beginner's luck who's upset the conceit of every hoary old gardener in the district?'

Striving to be equally reasonable, Chantal forced the stiff admission, 'Our garden is certainly a showpiece. You have green fingers, Peter, there's no doubt of that, and you enjoy your hobby—but that's all it is or ever can be—a hobby!'

She tensed for an explosion of wrath, but was instead surprised and a little shamed by his mature response. 'It's not a hobby to me, Sis, it's my life. To own a piece of ground, to dig, to hoe, to plant seeds and watch them spring to life, gives me more happiness and fulfilment than words can describe. I *must* have colour around me if I'm to thrive! Blue sky, golden sun, green leaves, rainbow petals, are as essential to me as the air I breathe. I'd wither and die in an office, Chantal! If I must have mud and slush, please let them be under my feet!'

Troubled thought kept her mind so completely occupied that the ringing of the doorbell caught her by surprise. She was lifting a tray of buns from the oven—having decided to be prepared in case their visitor should prefer to take tea—and almost tipped them on to the floor as she jerked her wrist upward to scan her watch. Two-fifteen! It *had* to be the Marquis! Whipping off her apron, she yelled out of the window to attract Peter's attention. 'He's here! Come out of the potting shed and make yourself presentable. Don't forget to wash your hands!'

She rushed to the front of the house, wishing she was less susceptible to argument and also to her brother's charm. In spite of having grave doubts, she had almost been won round to his way of thinking—but not quite. Hope still flickered, a hope that once face to face with a probably elderly marquis who would use both diplomacy and tact when pointing out the insurmountable difficulties that lay in the way of a novice attempting the job of an expert, Peter would reluctantly, but sensibly, abandon the whole idea.

Consequently, when the door was flung open, the man standing on the doorstep was startled by the sight of green eyes sparkling a welcome, a tremulous, half-smiling mouth, and a shapely head crowned by a coronet of hair the colour of ripe chestnuts, tilted backwards to encompass the whole of him.

'Mademoiselle Barry?' She jerked an involuntary step away from the man whose voice held all the warmth of cracked ice.

'Yes ... Yes,' she stammered, scrabbling desperately to rearrange in her mind the picture she had formed of a small, dapper Frenchman, black-haired, black-eyed and dark-skinned. The only dark thing about this man was his brow, beetled at that moment by a frown. All the rest of him was fair—a blonde blue-eyed, tight-lipped giant whose sabre-slim frame was sheathed in an expensive suit of silver grey.

'Are *you* the Marquis de la Roque?' She had not intended to sound so rudely abrupt.

Blue eyes betraying the merest *soupçon* of hauteur flickered across her hot cheeks before his stiffly-held head conceded a nod.

'My card, mademoiselle.' Gingerly, she accepted the crisp white oblong extended within two fingers. 'If you require further evidence of identification it can be supplied,' he added, seeming surprised by her hesitancy. 'One moment, I'll fetch more papers from my car ...' As he turned in the direction of a powerful automobile that seemed to be stretched half the length of the street, Chantal remembered her duties.

'That won't be necessary!' she gasped, made to feel oafishly ill-mannered. Then, pride rampant, she tossed her head and stepped aside to invite him stiffly. 'Please come in, monsieur.'

As soon as he did so, the small hallway seemed to shrink in relation to his size. Even the faded wallpaper lost its look of homely comfort and in contrast with his elegant presence adopted a tawdry air that had never before seemed evident.

Uncomfortably aware of eyes boring into her back, she led him into the sitting-room and indicated a chair, inviting him to sit.

Waiting politely until she herself was comfortably settled he sat down in her father's large, heavy armchair which immediately assumed Lilliputian dimensions. His attitude puzzled her. They were strangers, yet behind his polite façade she sensed contempt, not of his shabby surroundings, but of herself.

Lean brown fingers drummed upon the briefcase resting on his knee, a tattoo of impatience urging her on to speak. When she did not, his reluctance to remain a moment longer than was necessary was emphasised when he flicked back a spotless cuff to scan his watch then, in a tone that turned enquiry into condemnation, added,

'I believe you have a brother, mademoiselle. Is he not to join us?'

Peter replied for her by bounding into the room. 'Sorry about the delay,' he grinned, extending a welcoming hand, 'I presume you *are* the Marquis we were expecting?' In response to a brief nod, he rushed on. 'How do you do. I'm not quite sure how to address you, monsieur, we know so little about our mother's family. You could be one of our unknown relatives, in which case we'd have no need to be formal. I'm Peter, and my sister's name is Chantal.'

Whether the Marquis's action was deliberately snubbing Chantal could not guess, but when he rose to his feet to tower over Peter her brother seemed quite intimidated.

'No, we are not related. My name is Léon, Marquis de la Roque—but as our acquaintanceship is to be brief I suggest you continue using your chosen prefix.' Calmly he resumed his seat. 'And now that the matter of mode of address has been settled, perhaps, Mademoiselle Barry, *Monsieur* Barry,' his emphasis was insultingly strong, 'we may proceed with the business in hand?'

Feeling she had just been slapped across the face, Chantal stared, so angered by the rebuff she was incapable of speech.

Like a puppy that had received a cuff instead of an expected pat, Peter, red-faced with chagrin, slouched across to the couch. Casting an anxious look in Chantal's direction, he inched closer, taking

comfort from the fact that her fists were tightly
clenched, indicating that her temper was aroused
on his behalf. He suppressed a chuckle—like that of
all mild-mannered people, Chantal's ire was slow
to rise, but when it did it could be devastating!

He sensed that her teeth were clenched when, in
a voice that bore no similarity to her usual sweet-
sounding tone, she directed the insufferable marquis.

'We, too, are eager to have this meeting terminated as swiftly as possible, *monsieur*. As we know so
little, and you presumably are in possession of all
the facts, perhaps you would proceed to enlighten
us?'

His imperturbability was astonishing. Seemingly
oblivious to waves of animosity washing over him,
he unfastened his briefcase and withdrew a sheaf of
papers which he waved under their noses like a car-
rot with which to tempt a couple of hungry rabbits.

'You say you know nothing of your grandmother's
affairs and I am inclined to believe you,' he began.

'How very gracious!' Chantal grated.

His answering thrust was swift. 'Don't misunderstand me, mademoiselle. When I say that I believe
that you knew nothing of her affairs it does not follow that I believe you were unaware of her existence! I have no doubt whatsoever that had you
known the extent of her wealth you would have
been very eager to claim her acquaintance. In one
way, I suppose it could be said that you are partly
responsible for the accumulation of such wealth—it
is understandable, is it not, that a brokenhearted
woman, ignored and neglected by her family,

should throw herself into business in an attempt to assuage sorrow that would have swamped many a lesser person? To become rich was not her objective, wealth was merely a by-product of her grief. Yet it seems to me to be a great injustice that those who caused such grief should be allowed to benefit from it!'

The clear, cutting statements revealed his dislike and explained the cold reserve Chantal had recognised at their first moment of meeting. Her first instinct was to repudiate the charge of neglect he had levelled against her family and, conscious of Peter's start of surprise, she guessed that his impulse was to do the same. Instinct told her, however, that any protestations they might attempt would be ignored, so she forestalled Peter's impending outburst by laying a restraining hand upon his arm.

'Don't waste your breath arguing with the Marquis, Peter, he's obviously very well informed and will no doubt have collated very carefully all available information before pronouncing judgment. He's a thinker,' she smiled tightly, 'who has thought thoroughly and reached a very definite conclusion.'

Obviously undeceived by her honeyed tone, the Marquis threw her a narrow look. 'Are you accusing me of being a bigot, mademoiselle?'

'How could I possibly, monsieur,' she lanced sweetly, 'when, as everyone is aware, a dogmatic man is one guilty of profound ignorance!'

Two sharply indrawn breaths proved that she had scored a point—one from the Marquis whom she had rendered furiously angry, and the other from Peter who had never before heard acid sour the lips of his sweet-natured sister.

The Marquis was quick to recover. Shrugging the barb from his armour of self-assurance, he began in precise businesslike terms to outline the proposal he wished to put to them.

'As your solicitor has already explained, we—the Etablissement la Roque à Remi—wish to acquire outright ownership of the vineyard known as Trésor d'Hélène, which is situated in the area of the Falaises de Champagne. I believe that the price we propose to pay for this land is satisfactory to you both, therefore all that is required to conclude the deal is for each of you to attach your signature, where indicated, to these Agreements.'

'No, monsieur, that's not the only requirement.' No one was more surprised than Chantal when the objection sprang to her lips. 'My brother and I need time for further discussion before deciding how our inheritance is to be handled.'

'How it is to be handled ...' The rest of his sentence petered out on a puzzled breath. 'I don't understand—so far as I am aware the situation is an uncomplicated one: you want money, we want your land, a straightforward exchange hardly warrants lengthy discussion.'

'True ...' She managed a cool nod, struggling to hide her pleasure at his annoyance. 'But somewhere along the line, either you've been misled or you've jumped to an erroneous conclusion. You see, monsieur, the situation is not so cut and dried as you seem to imagine. It's quite possible,' she drew in a steadying breath, 'indeed, it's highly probable, that my brother and I might decide to run Trésor d'Hélène ourselves.'

Sensing Peter's tense jubilation, she outstared the Marquis, prepared for argument, for angry recrimination, but not for the shout of laughter that greeted her words. Furiously she waited, willing a tide of humiliated colour to recede from her cheeks. That his amusement was as genuine as his contempt was made obvious by the length of time he took to regain his composure. Grinning widely, teeth flashing white in a tanned face, he finally mustered sufficient control to deride:

'*Mes enfants*, if you truly are contemplating such a foolish step, I beg you to reconsider!'

'Why?' Peter's one demanding word drew the attention of the Marquis, whose head swung round to pinpoint bold blue eyes upon the boy's defiant face. What he read in Peter's expression must have communicated his determination, for every vestige of amusement disappeared from his face before, with a look that dared Peter to flicker so much as an eyelash, he spat the steely words:

'To one of normal intelligence the reason would be clearly obvious. However, as you seem unable to comprehend the utter folly of your proposal, let me outline to you some of the more obvious difficulties.

'It cannot be argued too strongly that the nucleus of a really good bottle of wine lies in the skill with which the grapes are grown. It is all too easy for some to make bad wine from good grapes, but only a miracle can change poor grapes into good wine. The Champenois wine-grower has perfected the art of viticulture, an art that calls for skill, patience, strong will, and the ability to overcome the many problems caused by our unpredictable northern climate, but it has taken him many centuries, during which time knowledge gained sometimes by chance, sometimes by mistakes, has been passed down from father to son to grandson. You may, in your ignorance have concluded that the cultivating of vines is as simple as farming in your own country. Nothing could be further from the truth. The vine must be cosseted, it is fussy about soil and climate, a hailstorm can set it back for weeks, it must have water when it needs it because it will show immediate resentment if it is left parched.

'So you see,' he sat back, his mouth curled into an indulgent smile, seemingly confident that his explanation would result in a satisfactory outcome, 'the odds against your achieving success as a winegrower are formidable.'

For the first time in her placid, uneventful life, Chantal was tempted to strike another human being, when the man she had decided she loathed picked up the offending Agreement and rustled the paper invitingly before advising with a patronage that set her teeth on edge.

'Stick to doing whatever it is you do best. You, mademoiselle, are a schoolteacher, I believe?' He smiled, prepared to be kind. 'In my opinion, it is a profession to which you seem ideally suited. And as for you, young man,' he turned to Peter, 'your future is crammed with endless possibilities, especially now that the money you are about to receive in exchange for your land can be used to further whichever career you eventually decide upon.'

A slim silver pen was thrust beneath Chantal's nose. 'As you are the elder, mademoiselle, you are entitled to the privilege of being first to sign.'

She sensed Peter mutely urging her not to give in, but she had no need of his guidance; already her mind was made up.

Ignoring the proffered pen, she rose to her feet, feeling surprisingly calm, surprisingly determined.

'I'm afraid my brother and I have caused you the inconvenience of a wasted journey, monsieur, for however much it might upset the plans of the Etablissement La Roque à Remi, we are neither of us prepared to forfeit our inheritance.'

'*Mon dieu!*' In one swift, lithe movement he was towering over her. 'You can't be serious!'

'*Mais oui, mon cher monsieur,* we are indeed serious,' she mocked solemnly.

His face darkened. In a voice stern as the cut of his suit, he spelled out coldly: 'Then you need expect no welcome in our province. The Champenois were passionately fond of your grandmother and are unanimous in their condemnation of the family whose neglect brought her so much grief. Casual visitors find it difficult to penetrate their natural reserve which is often mistakenly attributed to boorishness. Imagine, then, the reception that will be given to anyone who has offended against their code. Be warned, both of you, that if ever you should take up residence in Champagne every door will be closed against you, every face will be turned away!'

CHAPTER THREE

As the train rattled its way through a long valley Chantal turned away from the window to observe, 'What flat, boring countryside! I'd expected France to be exciting, *different*, but it's almost identical to home.'

'Which is hardly surprising,' Peter countered, 'when you consider how close the two countries are. If you want hot sun and golden beaches you must travel farther south; in Northern France the climate is much cooler, frost is just as likely to occur here as in England, at this time of year.'

Gloomily, she resumed her contemplation of miles upon miles of stark landscape nursing beds of sleeping vines, their bare, wizened branches sticking like skeleton limbs through a blanket of snow. She shivered, beginning to wish she had not allowed temper and a desire to thwart the wishes of an arrogant marquis to thrust her into an awkward situation which he had threatened would hold nothing but unfriendliness and strife should they be unwise enough to prolong their stay.

'I wish,' she addressed Peter in a small, troubled voice, 'we hadn't come.'

With a sigh of resignation he laid aside the book that had absorbed his attention throughout their flight to Paris and during the comparatively short journey by rail.

'Cheer up, Sis! It is January, remember, the worst possible time for pulling up roots and moving to a new home. Like the vines out there,' he nodded towards the window, 'your sap has run low, but in a few weeks it will rise with the temperature, buds of optimism will begin to sprout and roots will be put down, so that by the time spring arrives you'll emerge a strong healthy plant thriving in your natural environment.'

'If frost doesn't cast a blight over me first!' she shivered, pulling the hem of her coat closer around knees exposed to icy draughts.

He laughed, refusing to share her pessimism, 'There's less likelihood of frost on high ground than here in the valley. Look!' he pointed out of the window. 'There's the mountain where our vineyard is situated.'

Chantal twisted round to peer at a bulk that had appeared, towering hundreds of feet above the plain, its flat top capped by thick forest, its lush greenery gouged here and there by what looked like either ravines or quarries. Splashes of heather daubed the spaces between red-roofed cottages.

'Oh!' she exclaimed with surprise. 'I hadn't imagined we'd be living on the side of a mountain. Is it usual to find vineyards on such high ground?'

'According to this,' with a thumbnail Peter tapped the book he had been reading, 'those stretches of mountain vineyard are the prize vine-growing areas of the province. Seemingly, the *vins de la montagne*, as they're known, possess a highly developed vinosity that adds greatly to the quality of champagne.' He leant forward, his face earnest, and continued to impress his wide-eyed sister with knowledge gained from many hours of concentrated study.

'The most important stage in the manufacture of champagne is the preparation of the *cuvée*. Each House aims to produce a champagne of consistent flavour and quality year in, year out, despite the inconsistencies of the weather which can impose subtle differences upon each harvest. This is where the experience of the *chef de cave* plays an important part—it's he who has to prepare the *cuvée*, which is the selection of still wines he chooses to make up his blends.'

'But surely,' she frowned, 'each brand of champagne owes its taste and quality to the grapes of one particular vineyard?'

'Not at all,' he contradicted, 'the fruits of many different vineyards are employed. In the manner of an artist mixing paints, the *chef de cave* takes a little of this, a little of that, a *soupçon* of the other, experimenting, discarding, trying again, until a blend of perfect harmony is achieved. What I find interesting,' he told her thoughtfully, 'is that while studying the subject I discovered one important piece of information cropping up time and time again— that the area of the Falaises de Champagne is one in which the highest quality grapes are grown. Our vineyard, especially, is listed as *catégorie hors-classe*, which means that it's recognized as being one of the ten plum growths in the wine field province.'

He paused, awaiting some response, but when her expression did not alter he chided with suppressed impatience, 'Don't you see what this means? But perhaps not,' he forgave her hastily, 'I'm only just beginning to understand myself why the Marquis de la Roque was so eager to relieve us of our inheritance. For years the Etablissement La Roque à Remi has had exclusive access to a vineyard whose products are essential to the correct blending of their champagne. Without *our* grapes, the product that's made their name outstanding among the great champagne houses will never again achieve its legendary perfection. Our relatives, and the Marquis in particular, must find it galling that our grandmother who schemed so methodically to ensure that we didn't benefit from her riches should have allowed to escape her net the one commodity upon which the continued success of the House entirely depends!'

Chantal sank back into the cushioned seat, impervious to the rocking motion of the coach, her mind revolving with the speed of the wheels rushing the length of metal rails.

'No wonder he was furious when we refused to sell!' she gasped, her green eyes enormous. 'But surely,' she jerked upright, trying hard not to succumb to a heady sense of triumph, not to gloat too hastily at the prospect of seeing the haughty Marquis forced to bend a knee, 'there must be other vineyards where he could get the grapes he needs? You mentioned *ten* plum areas of growth ...' she faltered.

'And a dozen or so great champagne firms competing for the privilege of buying up their harvests!' he assured her swiftly.

While Chantal's brain was slowly evaluating this information she was startled by a sudden hoot of laughter. She looked up as Peter folded in his seat, convulsed with mirth.

'What's so funny?' she queried, half fearful, half amused.

'I've just thought of something,' he spluttered, 'something priceless ...! An absolute hoot ...!'

'Please share the joke!' she begged with an anticipatory gurgle.

'I've only just realised,' he gasped, fighting hard for control, 'that although the Marquis insisted that we couldn't win there's actually no way we can lose!'

Taking pity on her perplexity, he drew in a steadying breath, and spelled out slowly, 'The Etablissement La Roque à Remi depends upon the fruits of our vineyard for survival, Sis! *It can't afford to let us fail!* We're therefore in a position to demand whatever assistance we need without fear of refusal. The Marquis himself has stated that good wine can't be made from inferior grapes, so if he wants his wine to maintain its previous high standard he'll be forced to help me achieve my ambition to become one of the foremost viticulteurs in the province!'

Although the Marquis had been informed of their imminent arrival, there was no one to greet them when they stepped from the train, no vehicle of any description could be seen as they stamped the small draughty platform in an attempt to force circulation through frozen feet. It was no more than a temporary halt, so the train did not linger; mere seconds after they alighted it continued on its way, leaving them in solitary isolation on a concrete ramp exposed to an icy wind that seemed intent upon burying them and their luggage beneath piles of dead leaves.

'Come on,' Peter picked up the suitcases, 'that hut over there looks as if it might be a ticket office. With luck, it might be inhabited by one of our own species.'

The wizened face that popped up behind a glazed aperture after repeated knocking on an outer ledge did indeed look human, but a human wearing the sourest, most unfriendly expression Chantal had ever seen.

'Good afternoon,' Peter began politely, 'could you tell us where we could find transport to take us to Trésor d'Hélène?'

'*Parlez français?*' the old man snapped, clamping together jaws reminiscent of a steel trap.

Chantal's French, in fact, was very good indeed— but not wishing to put her brother in a humiliating position, she left the talking to him. As Peter began painstakingly explaining their needs in schoolboy French, she paced in an effort to keep warm, casting hopeful glances along the road that ran straight past the halt, curving and inclining gradually as it wove between fields of grey mud then plunged into undergrowth clothing the lower slopes of the mountain. She was peering upwards, wondering which one of the red-tiled houses dotting the slopes was theirs, when Peter stomped up behind her.

'Of all the obstreperous old curmudgeons!' he exploded with fury. 'Do you know, that old devil as good as told me to go back to where I came from! *No, there is no taxi service,*' he mimicked. '*No, the*

*bus service is infrequent; it will be two hours before
the next one is due!'* Then when I asked to use
his telephone to get in touch with the Marquis he
pretended he couldn't understand my French and
disappeared from the window! There's no doubt
about it, Sis, the Marquis has prepared the ground
well—that old devil knows who we are, and if his
unco-operative attitude is a sample of what we can
expect from the rest of the locals then we might
as well go straight back home.'

'We most certainly will not!' Chantal rounded
upon him. 'I had no wish to come here in the first
place, but now that I *am* here it will take more than
surly locals to drive me away. Don't you see, the old
man's attitude is part of a very well-thought-out
campaign! The Marquis means to get rid of us, to
make life so intolerable that we will be glad to sell
out and admit ourselves beaten. It's up to us to
show him how badly he's misjudged us by staying
put and fighting back, whatever the odds!' She
stooped to pick up a suitcase then, her back ram-
rod-stiff, she directed, 'Pick up that suitcase and
walk! Somewhere up there,' she nodded towards the
mountain mass, 'is Trésor d'Hélène. I intend to
arrive there before nightfall even if I have to *crawl!'*

After an hour of toiling ascent, she was ready to
eat her words. Both spirit and energy had begun to
flag. The road was steep, with an awkward camber that made walking difficult, its edges rough, un-
finished, littered with potholes and stones ranging
in size from marbles to boulders. Flinty slivers kept
finding a way inside her shoes—simple, medium-
heeled pumps that were ideal for travelling provided

one did not opt for travelling on foot!

Sensing her exhaustion, Peter nudged her elbow. 'Let's rest a minute.' He guided her in the direction of a fallen log. 'This looks large enough to take us both. Sit down before you collapse.'

Needing no extra coercion, she sank down on the log, then looked back along the road and gasped, 'Is that the roof of the railway station?' Her tone begged him to contradict. 'Surely not?' she wailed. 'It's only a stone's throw away—we *must* have walked farther than that!'

'I'm afraid not,' Peter sighed. 'All the twists and turns in the road put miles on the journey.' Suddently he stiffened, his eyes trained upon the descending road.

'What's wrong?' she questioned.

'Nothing … For a moment, I thought I caught a glimpse of a car rounding one of the bends.' He slumped back. 'I must have imagined it.'

Chantal shrugged, then stooped to take off a shoe, intending to remove a piece of grit that had been gouging agonizingly into her heel.

'Imagination be blowed!' Peter's yell startled her so much she dropped her shoe. 'It *is* a car! Come on, Sis, now's our chance to beg a lift.'

It was a superb automobile, a long, low-slung piece of mechanism that purred effortlessly to a halt in response to Peter's frantic wave. One dark red door was thrust open and as Chantal scrabbled for her shoe she caught a glimpse of plump upholstery and cream-coloured leather that twanged a chord of memory. Her dreadful suspicion was confirmed when a supercilious voice drawled far above her head.

'You seem to be in difficulty, mademoiselle, can I be of any help?'

'No, thank you.' Furiously she grabbed the offending shoe, slipped it on to her foot and jerked upright to glare at the thinly-smiling Marquis.

'We would be grateful for a lift!' Peter did not suffer the same proud inhibitions as his sister. 'We've walked for more than an hour without meeting a soul. Are we anywhere near Trésor d'Hélène?'

'The vineyard is tucked well out of sight; it will be impossible for you to find it without help,' the Marquis assured him. He reached towards a rear door and held it invitingly open. 'Get in, I'll take you there.'

'Don't bother,' Chantal tossed her flaming head, 'we'll manage.'

But to her chagrin Peter ignored her protest and shot into the back seat. Incensed by his lack of pride, she jerked away, intending to walk on alone, but was caught and held by an unkind grasp upon her elbow.

'You are being foolish, mademoiselle,' the Marquis told her in a voice hard as the flint she had removed from her shoe. 'Get in, don't allow that chip on your shoulder to be the cause of further blisters on your heel.'

To be forced to back down was bad enough, but her humiliation escalated when she slid inside the car and came face to face with a girl who had twisted round in the passenger seat to watch with keen, observing eyes. She looked no older than eighteen, a brown-eyed, black-haired beauty, expensively dressed, obviously precocious and, Chantal suspected, extremely spoiled.

That she was either very insensitive or lacking in diplomacy was evident when her faultless mouth curled at the edges as she condemned with a fastidious shudder.

'*Quel horreur!* How hot and dusty you both look—as if you have been tramping the roads for ever ...'

Chantal glared at the vision dressed in dusky pink, resenting the immaculate hairdo, the fascinatingly accented voice, the perfect make-up, exquisite nails manicured to the shape of almonds and tinted a slightly paler shade than her dress.

'Don't be unkind, Nicole.' The Marquis's censure was indulgent to the point of approval. 'Mademoiselle Barry,' he tossed across his shoulder as he prepared to start up the car, 'may I introduce to you my young cousin—Nicole Mortemart. Nicole, meet Mademoiselle Chantal Barry and her brother Peter.'

'*Enchantée!*' With a bored wave Nicole acknowledged the introduction, then turned her back, dismissing them as unimportant.

With temper flying high rags of colour in her cheeks, Chantal tried to relax as the car purred up the mountainside, but found it impossible to shake off the sense of inferiority conjured by the girl's expression of resentment of their intrusion, an expression which—aided by the flicker of an eyelash, the twitch of an elegant nose—had managed to reduce herself and Peter to the level of servants daring to impose upon the generosity of their betters.

'Why didn't you let me know you were coming?' The Marquis's concern sounded genuine. 'I would have met you at the station.'

Peter, who from the moment he had bolted inside the car had been unable to tear his eyes from Nicole's delectable profile, was shocked from his trance. 'But we did!' he blurted. 'I sent you a telegram.'

The Marquis frowned. 'I did not receive it,' he denied curtly. 'When was it despatched?'

'Yesterday morning, at ten o'clock,' Peter told him promptly. 'We'd planned to arrive unannounced, but at the last moment had second thoughts—hence the telegram instead of a letter.'

'Strange .. !' The Marquis's frown deepened.

'You think so, *mon cher*?' Nicole queried prettily. 'I do not. Have you forgotten how faithful our people are to the dear Comtesse's memory? How bitterly they resent the intrusion into their lives of relatives who ignored her existence? It is my guess, *chéri*, that the telegram was ... er ... mislaid, before it even left the post office.' She swung round to address a space above Chantal's head. 'You will discover that the Champenois are possessed of a loyalty as sturdy as their vines. They will neither forgive nor forget the taste of bitter wine.'

Unbearably goaded, Chantal retorted, 'Isn't it just possible that sometimes the bitterness present is not in the wine but in the mouth of the taster? I don't like forming hasty opinions, nevertheless it seems to me that the few Champenois I've met so far all appear to be suffering from a surfeit of sour grapes!'

The stunned silence that followed her words was broken by a shout of laughter. 'Bravo, mademoiselle!' The Marquis was grinning widely. 'That type of acid repartee is one in which your grandmother excelled. She would have been delighted to know that her granddaughter is a true Champagne Girl—all sparkle, wit, and fire.'

'And ready any second to pop her cork!' Peter muttered in an undertone so low that only Chantal overheard. To his relief she seemed to find his quip amusing; tension drained from her, she relaxed against the cushioned seat, the beginnings of a curve lifting the edges of her still-mutinous mouth.

Sensing, perhaps, that her verbal ammunition was inadequate against the fire of the red-haired English virago, Nicole retired into a cool shell, remaining completely silent while the car wended its way through neat, impersonal villages, not in the least pretty or picturesque, just rough plaster-covered walls, roofs of drab blue slate or occasionally of red tiles, and a total absence of paint on walls, doors and window frames.

The few inhabitants that appeared also impressed Chantal as being severely functional—men with brown, weather-beaten faces, their sturdy frames draped in muddy blue overalls; rosy-cheeked women, strong, buxom, and unsmiling, wearing well-washed aprons and shepherding clutches of equally well-washed children.

She had to acknowledge that in one respect at least the Marquis was right. On their own, they would never have managed to find Trésor d'Hélène, tucked away as it was, well off the beaten track with neither a signpost nor nameplate to aid any searcher.

'Is this it?' She could barely suppress her disappointment—dismay, even—when the car drove through a stone gateway flanked by wooden gates hanging drunkenly ajar. This house, if it was a house, appeared to be completely windowless, the symmetry of its bricks broken only by a small stone lintel accommodating the inevitable unpainted door.

Instead of braking, however, the Marquis swung the car around the side of the house and drew up in the middle of a courtyard offering a completely different aspect. From this angle the two-storied house looked attractive, even elegant. Flowered curtains fluttered at numerous windows, vines clung lovingly to outside walls, and many flower troughs edged the house, empty at present, but promising a riotous display of blooms during the spring and summer months. There was a garden full of shrubs surrounding a handkerchief-sized lawn, sheds waited to be explored, a greenhouse full of flowering plants and a garage with doors ajar exposing the bonnet of a small Fiat.

'Do you drive, mademoiselle?' The Marquis nodded towards the car.

'Yes, my father taught me,' she began eagerly, then, remembering her dislike of him, she hesitated, 'but as I've never driven on the Continent I doubt if I shall ever have sufficient confidence to make use of the car,' she finished abruptly.

'Just as well, then, that your visit is to be a short

one. Private transport is essential in this area unless one is prepared to live in complete isolation.'

There he goes again, Chantal fumed—implying that she and Peter were a pair of idiots who had to be humoured! The Marquis was certainly slow to admit defeat; even now, with feet firmly planted on their own ground and with suitcases packed with every article of clothing they possessed, his manner was that of a polite host welcoming a couple of casual visitors!

'Solitary confinement will suit us very well, monsieur. We've come here to work, not to be entertained. I expect we shall be far too busy during the coming months to make the acquaintance of even our nearest neighbours.'

'So!' The exclamation was terse. 'You really do intend to stay?'

'*Mais certainement*,' she tilted, reverting to his own language for an added touch of mockery. Then with pointed finality she extended her hand. 'Goodbye, monsieur, thank you very much for the lift, there's no need for you and Mademoiselle Mortemart to delay a moment longer.'

His head jerked back, as if reacting to a slap, but cold blue eyes did not waver from her face. Ignoring her outstretched hand, he lashed her confidence to ribbons.

'*Au revoir*, mademoiselle, not goodbye. I would prefer to leave you to your folly, but conscience will not permit it—if the blind insist upon leading the blind someone must be prepared to pull them out of the ditch.'

CHAPTER FOUR

JUST as the Marquis's car roared out of the courtyard a woman stepped from inside the house and remained with hands loosely clasped in front of her, silently waiting. As they approached the elderly woman her severe expression showed no sign of welcome. Dressed from neck to toe in black, her waist encircled by a leather belt supporting a bunch of keys, and with grey hair scraped into a tight bun exposing a profile that seemed chipped from granite, she looked formidable, an impassable *femme de charge*.

Even Peter's irrepressible spirits were doused by her obvious antagonism.

'*Bonjour*, madame,' he began soberly, 'my name is Peter Barry and this is my sister, Chantal. We're the new owners of Trésore d'Hélène.'

'*Usurpers!*' The venomous hiss chilled the blood in Chantal's veins. 'The Comtesse—God rest her soul—' swiftly the old woman crossed herself, 'will not rest easy while you both remain here!'

'Now just a minute...!' Peter reacted with heat.

'Be quiet, Peter!' Possessed of sudden dignity born of an intuitive recognition that the churlish old woman needed to be impressed, Chantal adopted a tone of authority. 'Am I right in assuming that you are the housekeeper, madame?'

'And have been so for many, many years!' The

old woman drew herself tall.

'Good.' Coolly, Chantal stepped past her. 'Then when you have shown us to our rooms you may return to your duties.'

The housekeeper stared. As Chantal had guessed, she had been a domestic all her life, from childhood she had been taught to respect authority, to react to it like a slave to the crack of a whip.

'Peter,' Chantal tossed across her shoulder as she sauntered towards the house, 'I'm dying for a wash and a change of clothes, would you mind bringing in the luggage?'

As Peter stooped to oblige, the housekeeper sprang into action. '*Non non, monsieur,* my son will do that! *Louis! Louis!*' She called out. '*Ici!*'

In response to her shout a man appeared in the doorway of one of the buildings and began shuffling his way across the courtyard. Curiously, Chantal eyed him, wondering why such a young, tall, superbly built man should be walking with dark head bowed and with such an awkward gait. He kept his eyes upon the ground and responded by sinking his chin further into his chest when his mother explained with appalling candour:

'My son is a *niais*—a simpleton, you understand. But a good worker,' she added with a fierceness that helped to vindicate her in Chantal's eyes. 'Though he cannot read or write, there is nothing he does not know about the art of viticulture.' Her last words were almost swallowed by an abrupt choke of pride that went straight to Chantal's heart.

Slowly she walked towards Louis who was stooping to pick up their suitcases. Placing a hand upon

his shoulder, she encouraged him upright and directed a dazzling smile into his brown, doe-gentle
eyes. 'How do you do, Louis,' she shook his hand.
'I'm so pleased to make your acquaintance, and I
know that my brother is just itching to pester you
with questions!'

His response was voiceless, a mute stare of adora-
tion that embarrassed her so much she was forced
to turn away. In search of diversion, she smiled at
his mother. 'May we know your name, madame?'

Tears that had welled into the housekeeper's eyes
were fiercely blinked away. Her expression remained hard, her mouth retained its tight unsmiling line, so that in contrast her voice sounded start-
lingly soft. 'Like your late grandmother, you are of
a *catégorie hors-classe, mademoiselle*. My name,' her
voice quavered, 'is Madame Budin, but the Comtesse always called me by my Christian name, which
is Hortense. I should be honoured if you and your
brother would do the same.'

The interior of the house was furnished and
decorated with a restraint that became apparent the
moment they stepped inside a hall with walls hung
with hunting trophies and engravings of local
country scenes. Upon a floor of octagonal tiles were
dotted chairs of wood and woven cane with floral
patterned seat cushions. In the living-room the
decor was a pleasant mixture of elegance and rus-
ticity, with checked blue and white curtains making
an unexpected contrast with a Louis XVI table and
matching chairs.

Chantal craned her neck to examine a ceiling
crisscrossed by ancient beams, then her attention

was caught by a fruitwood stand inset with Delft
tiles that had been utilised as a charming jardiniere.
Every corner of the house held some pleasant visual
surprise, unexpected forms of still life placed in
numerous nooks and crannies, beautiful Sèvres vases
and bowls glowing with colour against whitewashed
walls, watercolours depicting scenes of subdued
serenity.

Hortense preceded her up the stairs and flung
open the door of a room with a flourish. 'This,
mademoiselle, is the main bedroom, part of what
used to be the Comtesse's personal suite. I'm sure
you will find it comfortable.'

Chantal held her breath as she stepped inside a
room that was a veritable bower of roses. The same
rose-patterned print had been used to cover walls,
ceiling, bedcover, and one plump armchair placed
close to a window stretching the full height of one
wall. Porcelain table lamps with rose-coloured
shades were strategically positioned, one on the bed-
side table and the other on top of a writing desk
shining with the patina of old, polished wood. But
the outstanding feature of the room was a stove of
white *faience*, its decorative flue pipe recalling to
mind the funnel of a bygone steamboat. Carpet
flowed from wall to wall, thick and green as summer grass.

One errant piece of fluff had dared to float down
upon its surface. With a click of annoyance Hortense stooped to remove it, causing Chantal to smile
as she likened the old woman's action to that of a
child picking a daisy. When the housekeeper raised
her head she assumed the smile to be one of pleasure.

'Mademoiselle approves ... ?' she queried with an encompassing wave around the room.

'It's breathtaking,' Chantal sighed. 'I'm finding it difficult to equate such luxury with the austerity of the exterior. Approaching the house, one could be forgiven for mistaking it for a prison.'

'Ah, yes, there is a very good reason why we French keep hidden from view the true quality of the surroundings in which we live. Because of an iniquitous tax levied on all *signes exterieurs de la richesse* prudent householders take care never to parade their possessions before the public eye, so to speak. As the law now stands, it is a profitable thing —if one is wise—to appear poor even if one is rich.'

'I'm beginning to understand why the French have gained a reputation for thrift,' Chantal teased, her smile robbing her words of any sting.

Madame sniffed. 'It is true that we believe in practising economy, but never at the expense of comfort or taste. For instance, we French do not believe in merely eating—we must always dine.'

'Just as you must always be autocratic, individualistic to the point of being ungovernable, and oozing with conceit and self-confidence!' Chantal mentally registered, her thoughts upon one particular Frenchman.

The promise contained in the housekeeper's words was fulfilled to the hilt when later that evening they sat down to dinner. When Chantal had washed and changed into a dress of fine wool to combat the chill of the winter evening, she went downstairs to discover a table set for two in a small salon. Guided by the sound of pans rattling on a stove, she went in search of Hortense and found her in the kitchen about to sample the contents of one of many simmering copper saucepans.

Surprised by her entrance, Hortense swung round from the stove and lowered her tasting spoon. 'Dinner will be ten minutes or so, mademoiselle—just time enough for yourself and your brother to enjoy an aperitif.'

'That will be lovely,' Chantal smiled, 'but we'll wait until you and Louis are ready to join us. Where do you keep the cutlery, I'll set two more places at the table?'

'*Mais non*, mademoiselle,' Hortense protested, 'it is not *comme il faut* for servants to eat with their employers.'

Firmly Chantal quashed this notion beneath a determined foot. 'Now listen to me, Hortense, and listen well. My brother and I have not come here to play lord and lady of the manor, we have come to work. Trésor d'Hélène is to be our livelihood, we have no source of income other than what we expect to receive from the sale of our product, so a successful harvest is essential to us. Without the help of yourself and Louis we can't hope to survive.' Thoughtfully she traced the wood-grained table top with a fingernail. 'You see, Hortense,' she continued carefully, wondering if she was being wise, 'I'm laying all my cards on the table. Peter and I could pretend, try to bluff our way through, but honesty plays an essential part in any good relationship and we want to establish a team—you, Louis, Peter and myself, all working harmoniously together.'

She kept her eyes lowered, continuing her idle

tracing, but was inwardly tense as she awaited the old woman's response. Without her co-operation they were lost. Was the small breach they had made in her defences sufficient to overcome deeply-ingrained mistrust? Usurpers, she had called them —takers of possession without right. Was it foolish to hope for a change of heart from a woman whose views were as rigidly held as her backbone? Chantal chanced an upward glance and saw indecision written across the housekeeper's face. Worry-lines scoring deep into her forehead told of the struggle taking place between a flattered ego and family loyalty.

Suspecting she had lost, Chantal sighed and walked towards the door.

'*Un moment!*' She halted, hardly daring to hope, then feeling vaguely encouraged slowly turned around.

Hortense's dark eyes mirrored sombre decision. Loudly and firmly, as if to drown the voice of inner conscience, she stated, 'You have paid me the compliment of honesty, mademoiselle, therefore the compliment must be returned. I confess that when first I heard that the Comtesse's grandchildren were to inherit the vineyard I was dismayed, not just because the legacy ran contrary to her wishes, but also on Louis' account. I am getting old,' she straightened stooping shoulders, subconsciously decrying her own words. 'I was just fourteen years of age when I was taken into the d'Estrées household with the object of being trained to take over the duties of lady's maid to the newly-wed young Comtesse. During long, happy years of service your grandmother and I became very close——' she paused, her mouth working, then marshalled iron control in order to continue. 'In spite of the difference in station, we became friends and confidantes, rejoicing in each other's happiness, sharing each other's joys, having our friendship strengthened by the grief of bereavement when within the space of a few months we were widowed as a result of the war. Hard times followed for both of us, yet, sheltered as I was beneath the wing of my benefactress, I never once felt threatened—until now.'

Chantal's head jerked upward. 'Until *now?*' she stressed incredulously. 'You feel that Peter and I represent a threat?'

'Do not misunderstand me, mademoiselle,' the housekeeper's expression grew even graver, 'the Comtesse left me well provided for, I could move tomorrow into a cottage in the village and prepare to end my days in idleness. No, it is for my son's sake that I worry—Trésor d'Hélène is the only home he has ever known, every shovelful of earth is important to him, each individual vine receives from him the tender loving care of a mother anxious to rear a strong, healthy child. Such is his devotion to his work, he many times succeeds where others fail— which is why offers of work have poured from everywhere in the district. But for him to leave here would be tantamount to depriving him of his family and might result in disastrous damage upon his simple mind. Consequently, mademoiselle,' she admitted, her honest chin outthrust, 'though my true loyalty lies buried with the Comtesse, I feel forced to accept your offer.'

Chantal's gasp of relief filled the quiet vacuum left behind when Hortense lapsed into silence. Her acceptance had sounded like an admission of defeat, yet given sufficient time, she assured herself with soaring optimism, it should not be impossible to woo her on to their side. Obviously, Louis was her Achilles heel, which made it imperative for them to gain his allegiance. Once that had been achieved the Marquis could be completely routed!

A great deal of argument was needed before Hortense agreed to seal their contract with a celebratory glass of sherry. She remained adamant, however, that Louis and herself should continue to eat in the kitchen.

'My son would be nervous and ill at ease,' she excused. 'The very idea of eating with strangers would scare him half to death.'

Peter, whom Chantal had swiftly put in the picture, immediately intervened. 'I'll ask him, shall I? We've spent the past hour talking together and he did not seem the least bit put out by my presence. I have so much to learn, madame, that I must make use of every second Louis can spare. From him I hope to learn all there is to know about the art of viticulture.'

'*Alors!*' Hortense threw up her hands in a gesture of mock despair. 'That is the one conversation he will carry on until Doomsday! To every other subject he responds with grunts and snorts, but once vines are mentioned he becomes a veritable chatterbox.'

And so it turned out. Throughout a superb meal that began with an excellent onion soup, then progressed to chicken cooked in wine, terminating with a superb, deceptively creamy cheese with the kick of a culinary mule, Louis' voice droned in the background, his slow, gentle tone often hesitant when seeking for a particular word, but threaded through with an enthusiastic undertone.

'They seem to be getting on well,' Chantal smiled.

Still not quite at ease, Hortense swept imaginary crumbs from a spotless tablecloth. 'Your brother is good at putting people at their ease. In looks, he resembles his mother, but not in character—she was a shy, quiet girl, uncomfortable in the company of strangers.'

'You knew my mother well?' Even as she uttered the surprised question Chantal realised its superfluity. Undoubtedly, having lived as one of the family for so long, Hortense must have known her mother intimately.

'*Knew* her ... ?' The old woman bridled. 'Was I not present at her birth? Did I not nurse her through every childhood ailment, comfort her adolescent fears, and later was I not torn in two by her confidences about the young lieutenant who had swept her off her feet? I loved her as my own child, but I wronged her when I bolstered her hopes that the Comtesse might allow her to marry him. Just as I wronged my mistress by encouraging her daughter in her secrecy.' Her eyes clouded, her voice sank to weary depths, so that Chantal became aware that although the old woman was physically present her spirit had winged back to days long past.

'I never dreamt that the breach between them would be so prolonged,' she muttered almost to herself. 'Knowing the depths of affection they shared, how could I be expected to guess that bitterness would be allowed to separate them both for ever? With the passing of the years my conscience has eased, too much so, perhaps, for it seems that *le bon dieu*, in his wisdom, has sent images to remind me of my guilt—a girl who is a replica of her grandmother and a boy made in the image of his mother!'

Moved by intense sympathy, Chantal reached out to take her hand. 'You mustn't blame yourself, Hortense, you loved them both, they had no right to place such an intolerable burden upon your loyalty.'

This truth seemed to reach her. She raised her head to show thin lips almost, but not quite, stretching into a smile.

'You echo the sentiments of the Marquis, who assured me: "You are too straightforward to drive on a twisting road, Hortense. Absolve yourself of guilt by remembering that the Comtesse was a little too impulsive, a little too possessive, and far, far too lenient towards a daughter who, from all accounts, was a vain, wilful little fool." '

'How *dared* he make such remarks about my mother!' As Chantal's head shot up, light from an overhead lamp endowed her hair with a thousand fiery sparkles. 'By what right does he presume to sit in judgment?'

Hortense began gathering up the used dishes. That she considered the matter trivial was evident when in a matter-of-fact voice she consoled, 'The Marquis was merely repeating an opinion he has heard expressed from childhood. His father and your mother were betrothed before she eloped with her lieutenant. Because he wished for an heir, his father did eventually marry, but it was a marriage without love, so far as he was concerned. Fortunately for his bride, she died young, but I have always felt pity for the son left behind to bear the brunt of his father's bitterness. Many times over the years I have tried to repair the damage done to your mother's reputation, to rid him of misguided opinions passed down to him from his father, but without much success. You must try not to let his attitude upset you, mademoiselle,' she sighed, 'it will help you to forgive if you bear in mind the fact that throughout his boyhood the Marquis was taught to regard the name of Camille d'Estrées as being synonymous with selfish, cold-blooded deceit.'

CHAPTER FIVE

'WE have a problem, Chantal!' Peter's young face looked grave. They had been at Trésor d'Hélène for two weeks, a period which to Chantal seemed no less than a couple of hectic, hard-working months.

Louis and his mother were strict taskmasters. Hortense, although her actual activities were confined to the house, planned out their work programme with the efficiency of a general deploying his troops. Each morning she demanded of Louis: 'How are the vines progressing?' and listened carefully to his detailed reply. The short winter rest during which the vines slept was almost over, and each week brought further indications that they were about ready to stir into life.

The whole of the previous week had been spent freeing vine shoots from the wire to which they had been attached the previous spring—a job so backbreaking that by the time all the short pieces of straw had been removed and burnt in order to destroy any harboured pests, Chantal felt she had developed a hinge in her back that creaked and groaned each time she bent or straightened.

This morning Hortense had directed her usual question. 'How are things, Louis?'

'Fine, Maman,' he had told her with slow, careful diction. 'The shoots are all untied; the water stops have been dug.'

'Good!' It was hard to decide when Hortense was pleased, because her expression seldom altered. Yet she somehow conveyed satisfaction in her sharp instruction, 'It is now time for the *épandage des fumiers.* We will require extra hands—go down to the village and fetch two of our usual helpers.'

'*Oui*, Maman.' Louis had risen from the breakfast table to collect a ramshackle bicycle from one of the sheds then he had cycled off towards the village. Half an hour later, as she washed up the breakfast dishes, Chantal had seen him return.

She stacked the last of the plates and turned with sinking spirits to face Peter who was lounging dejectedly on the threshold. 'What sort of trouble?' she questioned lightly, determined not to become embroiled in his tangle of adolescent emotions—one minute elated, the next in the depths of despair.

'The local men are refusing to work for us. According to Louis, the same workers turn up here year after year in search of casual employment. He was surprised at having to go in search of them, being experienced workers they know as well as he what jobs are to be done, and when. When he eventually ran them to ground they refused point-blank to work for us. Apparently, everyone in the village is of the same mind—not only are they opposed to us, but Madame Hortense and Louis are also to be ostracised. Because they're helping us, the villagers have labelled them traitors, disloyal to the memory of their late patroness.'

'Oh, hell!' With a vexed grimace Chantal ran angry fingers through her hair. 'The Marquis de la Roque is responsible, of course,' she fumed. 'His strategy is obvious—without assistance the work can't be done, so we'll be forced to appeal to him for help—which will be readily given, providing we agree to sell out!'

'But, Sis,' Peter protested, 'a successful harvest is as important to him as it is to us!'

'I'm beginning to doubt that!' she snapped. 'The devious Marquis must have prepared his ground well. One bad year will break us, but will it break him? Obviously not, or he wouldn't be prepared to leave us to flounder!'

'You could be right.' Peter gave a soundless whistle of dismay. 'Each year at least one eighth of the new wine is put into reserve, so he's bound to have stocks to fall back upon.'

'The cunning devil!' Peter stared at his normally placid sister, whose vocabulary was becoming libellous. 'Then there's nothing else for it—we must manage alone. I'm determined that insufferable brute will not get the better of us!'

'Have you any idea what you're letting yourself in for?' Peter choked. 'The *épandage des fumiers* is no job for a woman!'

Without waiting to translate, she told him fiercely, 'The job can be no more menial or back-breaking than those I've tackled these past two weeks. Lead the way! Whatever form the work takes I'll do it!'

Half an hour later she was fighting to suppress waves of nausea while she forked manure into bags to enable Louis and Peter to carry it to the vineyard where it was to be spread along channels carved out between rows of vines. Gritting her teeth, she

plunged her fork deeply into the decaying mass, trying not to worry about how she was to rid her
clothes, skin and hair of a stench so pungent it
seemed to have seeped into every pore.

Louis had registered horror when her decision
had been communicated to him. '*Mais, non, mademoiselle!*' he had protested, before appealing to
Peter in stumbling haste. Peter had listened patiently, then after Louis had stomped away, still muttering dissent, he had pleaded uncomfortably:

'Look here, Sis, I've just been made to feel
whatever's the present-day equivalent of the old-
fashioned cad. Louis seems to blame *me* for the fact
that you're even within sniffing distance of that
stinking muck. Unfortunately, he was unable to obtain a supply of local manure which I gather is comparatively sweet-smelling compared to this—the
droppings of cows and sheep, dead leaves, pressed
grape skins, vegetable matter and the like—so he
had to resort to buying *les boues de la ville de Paris*
which, believe it or not, consists of the contents of
Parisien dustbins. It's brought here by rail in sealed
tanks, but only during autumn—in warm weather
the stuff becomes so ripe that even the locals protest.'

Chantal stopped bagging just long enough to
direct one fiery question. 'When Louis said there
was no local manure available did he mean there
was none at all or that there was none available for
us?' He nodded briefly, confirming her suspicion.
'Very well,' as she stooped to pick up the fork he
caught a glimpse of a very determined jaw, 'let's get
on with our work.'

Hortense brought them coffee and sandwiches for lunch, then, wrinkling her nose in disgust, she scurried back to the house. Chantal, who found it impossible to eat, had to turn away from the sight of Peter and Louis wolfing down bread that had been contaminated by smell the moment the sandwiches were unwrapped. Even her coffee tasted repugnant and was emptied on the ground after one tentative sip.

It was almost nightfall by the time they had finished. Feeling little elation, they stood regarding the fruits of their labour—rows of vines, their sparse branches rearing high as if anxious to outreach the stench of rotting garbage striping the vineyard. Odd bits of newspaper floated on the breeze; cigarette packets, cardboard cartons, vegetable peelings and many other items of household rubbish that by rights ought to have been ground to extinction by the suppliers, lent the appearance of a rubbish dump to the once tidy plots.

'Don't feel despondent, Sis.' Peter sounded as cheerless as she felt. 'In a few weeks this lot will have decomposed and will look exactly as manure should. Let's get back to the house. I hope Hortense has delayed dinner, because I intend to spend at least an hour in a steaming, antiseptic bath!'

Chantal could not have been more in agreement. She felt bone weary, aching all over, her face and hands streaked with dirt, her most dilapidated jeans and oldest jumper daubed with blobs of revolting, smelly goo. Every stitch she had on would go straight into the dustbin, she promised herself as she followed the others down a narrow lane, feeling grate-

ful that at least there was no one about to witness
their discomfiture.

The thought had no sooner registered when the
sound of horses' hooves warned of a rider's approach
—two riders, she noted, scrambling aside into a
deep patch of dusk. Her heart jerked at the sound of
a girl's laughter, then, when a familiar masculine
voice replied, she felt an urge to throw herself into
an accommodating ditch.

'Well, well, what have we here?' The Marquis
reined in his horse to stare down at her, openly
amused.

'*Quel horreur!* Brut, what is that obnoxious
smell?' Nicole peered through the dusk. 'Mademoiselle Barry?' she questioned on a high note of incredulity. 'It surely cannot be ... ?'

Simultaneously the Marquis and Nicole burst
into laughter. Not one whit put out, Louis and Peter
stood grinning sheepishly, enjoying the joke at their
own expense. But the humour of the situation entirely escaped Chantal. Nicole was, as usual, immaculately dressed in riding clothes tailored to hug
the seductive contours of her lithe young body. A
peaked riding cap lent to her face the look of a
cheeky infant, but there was no childish innocence
contained in the words she addressed supposedly to
the three of them but which Chantal guessed were
aimed exclusively towards herself.

'Honest labour bears a grimy face,' she trilled,
'but must it be accompanied by such a revolting
smell?'

'Don't condescend!' Chantal was appalled by the
surliness of her own voice. 'There's no shame in

hard work, why don't either of you try it some time? But then half a day would probably kill you ...'

When a deluge of tears began aching behind her eyes she knew it was time to make an escape. Ill-mannered though it was, she stalked off with her nose high in the air, grateful for gathering dusk that cast a veil of secrecy over her tear-stained cheeks.

But she was not fated to escape so easily. At the sound of following hoofbeats she began to run, but was cornered by her tormentor when she had to stop to fumble with the fastenings of a gate stretching the width of the lane. She had opened up a space almost wide enough to slip through when a hand grasped the top bar and banged the gate shut. She whirled to face him and, dangerous as a trapped vixen, spat out her resentment and scorn.

'Why do you follow me, monsieur? To gloat upon the results of your campaign? You may have reduced me to the level of the dung-heap, but I'm by no means on my knees!'

Leisurely he dismounted, leant an elbow on the gate, then bent closer to peer into startled green eyes.

'Tears ... ?' The softly spoken word teemed with questions she was not prepared to answer. When he reached out a finger to detach a crystal drop from her lashes she jerked from his touch as if scalded. 'There is a sweet sort of sadness in tears; are you sad, mademoiselle?'

'Would it gratify your abominable conceit if I were?' She had to whip up anger to combat an inner riot caused by his false tenderness. 'A woman's tears can also be activated by temper,' she reminded him fiercely.

'Why are you angry?' He seemed determined to humour her, to act the part of a benevolent *patron*. Chantal found his hypocrisy sickening.

'Why ... ?' She almost choked on the indignant word. 'You curtail our supply of local manure so that we have to resort to using the contents of filthy dustbins, you command the locals not to work for us so that we're forced to do the whole of the work ourselves, then, to complete your satisfaction, you turn up here, choosing your moment well, in order to gloat and *laugh* at us—yet you have the *gall* to ask me why I'm angry!' It was obvious that of all the charges she had laid at his door she considered his unkind amusement the most rankling. She glared up at him, incensed by a suspicion that he was once again having difficulty in suppressing a smile.

Yet his features were composed, his voice pelt-smooth, when he apologised, 'I'm sorry if you found my amusement hurtful, it was not meant to be. We Champenois possess a sense of humour so peculiar strangers can seldom appreciate it. A need to laugh is our outstanding characteristic, laughter rises within us like the bubbles inside a bottle of champagne and is dispersed just as quickly. But our laughter is never deliberately unkind, never meant to hurt. Believe me, mademoiselle, though we are a dour, unsociable, rather cruel-tongued race, we do possess one redeeming feature known as *la douceur Champenoise*—a sweetness to temper the sour.'

Close knowledge of her brother's nature made it possible not to contradict, for Peter had inherited all the traits the Marquis had outlined—though voluble, he spoke softly, seldom raising his voice; his movements were invariably slow yet in his steady fashion he accomplished much. He, too, had a wit that stung, but like a bee, once he had disposed of his small amount of venom he went winging on his way, thoughtlessly unconcerned.

Consequently there was less heat than she wished in her barb. 'Are you attempting to excuse your actions by implying that you are less wrong-minded than thoughtless, monsieur?'

'I am trying to make you understand my first re-action to the sight of a dejected scaramouche wend-ing her way home after labouring all day on a task that most men would find daunting. Custom de-crees that men may not weep,' he jerked, his tone developing a hard ring, 'which is why, had I not laughed, I might have communicated my dis-pleasure in a much more physical fashion.'

His unexpected hint of concern left her flounder-ing in a morass of confusion. She took a step away from him, hoping to quell pounding heartbeats, to control blood that was gushing through veins with the effervescence of champagne reacting to a cork popping from a bottle. She stared through the deep-ening dusk, green eyes sparkling resentment of the intoxicating emotions laying siege to her abstemious soul. Had she sipped some devil's wine? Succumbed to some devilish spell?

She glimpsed a hint of satanic satisfaction in eyes blue as newly-kindled flame that pierced the dusk, noting every nuance of uncertainty, dismay and confusion on her expressive features. That she was no match for his sophisticated brand of dalliance was driven home to her when he reached out a finger to poke inquisitively inside a dark red curl.

'*Belle châtaigne,*' he murmured, gently uncurling the burnished ring then laughing under his breath when, as he withdrew his finger, the fiery lock sprang back into its original coil. 'A golden head, a throat that purrs, eyes that put emeralds to shame, a perfect body that compels fierce undeniable attraction,' he whispered into her astonished ear. When his hands grasped her shoulders she remained stiffly rooted, her young mind awhirl, her naïve emotions defenceless against such sensuous barrage. '*Ma petite belle châtaigne,*' he whispered, touching cool lips against her downcast lashes, 'I am utterly perplexed—are you ice or fire? Are you Madonna or Magdalen?'

Chantal never quite knew what snapped the taut thread between them, it might have been the pad of restless hooves or the call of a bird passing overhead, but suddenly she became aware of the incongruity of the suave, immaculate Marquis seriously attempting to seduce a grubby, smelly urchin. A bubbling well of laughter opened up inside her and she folded up, giving rein to her amusement.

He jerked upright, affronted, and gladly she grasped the opportunity to extract revenge upon the tall, blue-eyed boss man of the vineyards, whose conceit had led him to expect her to be as available as the bunches of luscious grapes that fell so readily into his hands.

Had she been born a full-blooded Champenoise, she could not have poured more scorn upon his folly. 'Thank you, monsieur, for helping to restore my sense of humour. According to Hortense, who I must admit has little regard for the opposite sex, the men of this area are,' she began ticking off on her fingers, 'cuckolds, beggars, toads and asses. You seem to me to epitomise all of their attendant vices. Did you really think you could override my contempt of your despicable tactics by muttering a few compliments in my ear?' She stamped a foot in her rage. 'Couldn't you have done justice to my intelligence by at least choosing a more appropriate moment?' Grabbing an odorous handkerchief from her pocket, she flung it straight into his face.

'*Mon dieu ...!*' Instinctively he recoiled.

'*Quel horreur!*' She mimed Nicole's theatrical shudder, then braved blazing blue eyes just long enough to mock. 'I pity you, monsieur—as I would pity a snake-charmer bitten by his own snake!'

She ran all the way back to Trésor d'Hélène and burst into the kitchen, startling Hortense into dropping a handful of spoons back into the cutlery drawer. 'Please delay serving dinner for half an hour,' she begged, 'I must rid myself of this smell.'

'Gladly,' the housekeeper's nose wrinkled. 'Fortunately there are two bathrooms—your brother is already occupying one of them.'

As she mounted the stairs Chantal heard Peter singing at the top of his voice and wondered what had brought about such a quick change of humour. But then the necessity to feel sweet and clean again took precedence. First of all she shampooed and thoroughly rinsed her hair, then she luxuriated in a bath filled with pine-scented water, soaping every

inch of her skin, scrubbing beneath her nails, until
all that remained of the *épandage des fumiers* was
a ghastly memory.

She thought herself composed when she sat down
at the dinner table, yet Peter's opening remark
caused an inner nerve to jerk.

'You and Brut seemed to find plenty to say to one
another?' The statement was more a question.

Nodding approval of the generous helping of
pâté Hortense was heaping on to her plate, she took
time to quell her emotions before prevaricating.

'Brut ... ?'

'The Marquis,' he enlightened crossly, showing
his dislike of pretence.

Determined not to be drawn until such time as
she could reflect upon the interlude without pain or
tremor, Chantal further incensed him by idly re-
flecting.

'Brut ... The name is certainly applicable!'

Hortense surprised them with one of her rare
chuckles. 'The word has an extra meaning to us—
one that is probably unknown to you. Brut is a
category of champagne, the very driest variety that
is always drunk at the beginning of a meal, never at
the end because fruit and sweet desserts paralyse its
delicate flavour. The Marquis' name is actually
Léon, but his friends, when they rechristened him,
obviously had in mind his natural acidity. Predictably, even his taste in women runs towards the
elegant and sophisticate rather than the sweet
ingenue.'

'That can hardly be so, madame.' When Peter
contradicted in a soft, dreamy voice Chantal paused

in the act of transferring a morsel of pâté to her mouth to stare at her unfamiliarly sober-looking brother. 'He's very fond of his cousin, Nicole, and she is the sweetest, most gentle girl I've ever known. Don't you agree, Chantal?'

Chantal was shocked to see how vacant his stare had become. Suspecting a case of besotted calf-love, her reply was impulsive and foolish. 'As a tiger cub is gentle!' she wasped, then could have immediately bitten off her tongue. Quickly she attempted to repair the damage her sarcasm had caused, but Peter, whose appetite had always been his main consideration, rose from the table, cast her a look of injured disgust, then stalked out of the room.

Nonplussed, Chantal and Hortense shared a puzzled look.

'*Oh, là, là!*' the old housekeeper smiled broadly, 'the boy is obviously in love!'

Icy fingers clutched Chantal's heart and squeezed hard. Peter was not in love, she told herself, he was infatuated, and by a girl who had deliberately set out to charm him, just as her cousin had tried to charm herself. They must have plotted together— the Marquis and his cousin—to devise a scheme of planned seduction, to what end she could not guess, but intuitively she sensed that family harmony was being threatened. So long as she and Peter remained united they would be safe—separated, they would become vulnerable as lambs astray in a jungle.

CHAPTER SIX

TINY puffs of smoke were floating up into the soft spring sunshine. March had arrived, the best month of all for vines to be pruned. In every vineyard women and children were following in the pruners' footsteps, collecting the discarded shoots that were destined to be destroyed by burning on the many small bonfires.

At Trésor d'Hélène, however, there were no women or children evident, only a solitary, slender girl toiling in the wake of two men, one expertly wielding secateurs, the other paying rapt attention while his teacher instructed and demonstrated.

'Of all the vineyard tasks,' Hortense had explained earlier that morning, 'the pruning of the vines is the most important and, except for grafting, is the one requiring the most care and knowledge. In order to grow grapes of high quality it is important to restrict the number of bunches; a vine left unpruned will produce heavy crops, then quickly become exhausted.'

The air was still slightly crisp, yet perspiration was running in rivulets down Chantal's aching back. Grimly determined not to complain, she continued clearing the debris left by Louis' swift, sure secateurs and the smaller piles contributed by Peter, his carefully methodical pupil.

At the sound of approaching footsteps the three

of them looked up. Chantal's nerves tingled a vibrant warning when she recognised a tall figure, with uncovered head glinting golden in the sunshine, eating up yards of ground with long, athletic strides.

'It's Brut ... !'

Peter's familiar form of address incensed her, but not half so much as the welcome extended to the Marquis by the two men. With almost servile humility Louis doffed his woollen cap.

'*Bonjour*, Monsieur le Marquis!' he struggled shyly, then grabbed his secateurs, eager to retreat into the world he knew best.

Peter grinned. 'Nice of you to pay us a visit.' Then showing that he had inherited a truly Gallic lack of emotional inhibition, he looked beyond his shoulder, then quizzed with evident disappointment, 'Have you come alone?'

The Marquis was quick to supply the information he sought. 'Nicole and her mother have gone to Paris on a shopping expedition that is planned to last a few days.' He smiled briefly. 'However, if their previous expeditions are anything to go by, the visit will be extended until at least the end of the week. According to my young cousin, every item in her wardrobe is either out of date or shabby. I tell her that if all her clothes are in a worn state it would seem to indicate that she goes out too much.' His attention swiftly fell upon Chantal. 'What about you, mademoiselle?' The blue eyes seemed to pierce her through and through. 'Do you have the same problem?'

Acute self-consciousness made her sound abrupt. 'Parties are usually held to rid people of their social

obligations. We're too tired in the evenings to enter-
tain and even if we were not, adverse propaganda
has ensured that none of our neighbours would
accept an invitation to visit Trésor d'Hélène. Consequently, they feel no obligation towards us.'

Anxious to continue with his work, Peter excused
himself and hurried to join Louis who had advanced
a fair distance away.

Caught on the hop by his abrupt departure, Chantal found herself alone with the man, looking surprisingly at home in jeans that encased his narrow
hips and sinewed thighs in a tough denim skin.
Muscled forearms, tanned as leather, stood out
against the stark whiteness of a short-sleeved tee-
shirt of fine cotton that clung to his broad chest and
imparted a tigerish grace to every muscled movement. Exposed to a virility that had lurked unsus-
pected beneath his usual outfits of impeccable
formality, she turned aside to hide confusion and
with a muttered apology resumed her gathering.

A hand shot out to grasp her by the elbow. 'Leave
that!' he ordered sharply. 'I want to talk to you.'

Resentfully she tugged out of his grasp. 'You
may have time to waste, monsieur, but I don't. As
you can see,' she flung out an arm to encompass the
vineyard, 'the locals dare not offend you, so we're
having to do all of the work ourselves.'

'I will help you out,' he brushed her anger aside,
'but first of all you must listen to what I have to
say.'

'*You* will help us...!' Her incredulity was insulting.

His face darkened, eyes blue as chipped ice pinpointed in a look that froze the hot rush of blood coursing through her veins. Then, slightly mollified by her expression of white-faced fear, he threw back his head and laughed. 'Do I really give an impression of being incapable of a hard day's work?' he grinned. 'Believe me, mademoiselle,' he hesitated, frowned, then queried politely, 'may I call you Chantal?' Taking her assent for granted, he continued, 'No Champenois, whatever his ultimate status in life, is allowed to spend his boyhood in idleness. In common with those children,' he nodded towards a neighbouring vineyard, 'I was taught at a very early age the proper way to untie shoots, to dig water stops, to lay new earth, to apply manure,' his lips twitched, 'to prune, to spray, to trim, to become expert, in fact, in every stage of culture before I was even allowed inside the laboratories to learn the art of making champagne. So you see,' his teasing tone did strange things to her heartbeats, 'having served a hard apprenticeship I am perfectly well qualified to help you out. Should I become exhausted by the unaccustomed labour, however,' the twinkle in his eye grew brighter, 'I shall expect you to cool my fevered brow.'

The hint of irony, the slightly jeering, slightly accented voice had the infuriating effect of making her tremble at the knees. In her weak, uncertain state Chantal was no match for the charm he was spreading thick enough to bury her. Her salvation lay in the fact that his conceit had not allowed him to guess that she could see through his attempt to disarm a member of a family his father had taught him to distrust. That he was even bothering to talk to her indicated some ulterior motive, so, working on the premise that to be forewarned is to be fore-armed, she decided to play him along in the hope that she might gain some hint of the true purpose behind his devious manoeuvres.

'I'm ready for a rest.' She abandoned her task to direct him a dazzling smile. Praying he would not sense the inner havoc that was driving her pulses frantic, she held out her hand. 'Let's find some place to sit—for only ten minutes or so, re-member!' Pride retched at the necessity to deploy coyly swept-down lashes. 'Then afterwards you must stand by your promise to help me catch up.'

Incredibly, he was completely deceived. Captur-ing the hand she offered inside fingers of steel, he led her to a vantage point where, utilising an up-turned crate as a seat, they sat looking down upon slopes of terraced vines, a patchwork of plots each as coveted, as jealously guarded, as well maintained, as a demanding mistress.

'Remind me to bring you here at dusk some summer's evening,' he murmured in the seductively accented voice she found fascinating. 'Then, the subtle harmony of ochre-red tiles, blue-grey slates and the many-toned greens of vineyards, woods and fields creates a magic softness reminiscent of a Monet masterpiece. In early June the vines flower. Flower-ing starts at the bottom of the vine,' casually, his finger began tracing a line of fire from her wrist up the length of her arm, 'where the flow of sap is stronger, then spreads upwards. The yellowish green petals exude a heady scent that has been likened to that of the passion-fruit flower. Lovers wander the vineyards at sundown, when the scent is most potent, hoping to test out the claim that it is an aphrodisiac. We must join them, you and I, and try to discover for ourselves whether or not the legend is true.'

Chantal wanted to edge out of reach of the conscience-lacking Frenchman whose voice was purring wicked lies, whose brilliant eyes were sparkling with empty promises, whose charm was accomplished enough to render an aphrodisiac superfluous. In fact, she thought wildly, faced with the prospect of his close proximity in surroundings such as he had outlined, any girl with her wits about her would opt for the calming influence of a sedative!

'What ...' She cleared a nervous croak from her throat and began again. 'What was it you wanted to talk to me about?'

Mercifully, he abandoned pretence in favour of sobriety. 'You have levelled some unjust accusations against me. No amount of argument will convince you that I am innocent of these charges, therefore I propose to supply actual proof that I have never sought to influence the locals against you or your brother. Suspicion of strangers, resentment of newcomers, is too deeply ingrained in the Champenois for their attitudes to change overnight. Nothing I could say would make any difference, they will not be coerced. They might, however, be prepared to follow my lead, so what I am proposing is this. With your permission, and that of your brother, of course, Nicole and I will visit you often. We will hold out a visible hand of friendship by helping in any way we can to ensure the success of the vintage. Socially, too, you must be seen to have been accepted, and what better way to begin than by attending a ball that Nicole and her mother have arranged to hold in the Château? It is in aid of one of their pet charities, so everyone of note in the district will be attending. Once you have been introduced, invitations will follow. The Champenois labourer is a terrible snob —once he sees that you have been accepted by society you will have no further trouble finding workers for your vineyard.'

Chantal was not fooled. Luckily, he was unaware that Peter, with uncanny perception, had summed up the situation and concluded that the Marquis was worried about the quality of the forthcoming vintage and that by fair means or foul he would devise some means of ensuring its success. To allow him freedom to come and go as he pleased meant having to endure his overbearing arrogance, accept his expert authority, and having to carefully sift his every devious word. Yet his aim was their aim, therefore, in order to survive another year it made sense to accept his offer, to pretend to be deceived in order to gain the benefit of an extra pair of hands.

To mix socially with the Marquis, however, was an entirely different matter.

Looking suitably subdued, she brushed twin fans of gold-tipped lashes across flushed cheeks before stammering,

'It ... it seems we've misjudged you, monsieur. Your offer to help out is very generous, in the circumstances. On Peter's behalf, and my own, I accept gladly.'

In case his satisfied glint should overcome her temptation to smack his face, she clasped her hands tightly in her lap.

'And what about the ball?' he asked? 'Will you attend?'

'I'm ... I'm not so sure about that. I've nothing suitable to wear, I'm afraid.'

Pleased with the result of his performance, he threw back his head and laughed. 'Woman's age-old excuse!' he jeered. 'If she does not wish to attend a party she suddenly discovers that she has nothing to wear, just as, with equal ease, she can conjure up a headache from nowhere in order to avoid having sex!'

Wishing to conceal her flaming cheeks, she turned her head aside. 'On the first count you're being unfair,' she mumbled, 'many times in the past I've had to refuse invitations because, being a comparatively poor family, we had no money to spare for extravagant clothes. On the second count,' she hesitated, gulped, then galloped on, 'I've had no experience, so I can't pass judgment.'

'No experience ...!' he mocked. 'How old are you—twenty, twenty-one ...?'

'Twenty-two,' she croaked, humiliated by his obvious disbelief.

'I know the English are not renowned for their passionate natures,' he reached out to turn her face towards him, 'but you are half French, the daughter of a woman who I've been told was very expert in exploiting all the advantages woman holds over man. Don't tell me,' his mouth developed a snide twist, 'that she did not pass on to her daughter the secret of her success?'

Chantal faced his sardonic stare with wide, honest eyes. 'My mother died giving birth to Peter,' she told him simply.

For a second longer his blue eyes continued to jeer, then slowly they darkened as he took in the sense of her words. This time it was he who was nonplussed.

'I beg your pardon, Chantal. Please believe me. I had no idea ...'

'Didn't Uncle James explain our circumstances?' she queried, eyebrows raised.

'My discussion with your solicitor was run on strictly business lines,' he assured her stiffly, wrestling with the unfamiliar experience of being made to feel gauche, an awkward, insensitive brute.

Feeling she had had a brush with a tiger and was now holding him by the tail, Chantal could afford to be generous. 'Think no more of it,' she replied, full of sweet forgiveness. Before her triumph became too obvious, she jumped to her feet and reminded him, 'Come along, we've wasted enough time, how about that help you promised me?'

Chortling inwardly, she strode away, very aware of the subdued, deflated Marquis following in her wake.

It was a long time before she felt able to relax, to feel completely at ease working side by side with the man whose superb fitness showed in the manner in which he stooped and stretched, then stooped again for prolonged periods, working easily and swiftly along the rows of vines, displaying not the least hint of strain.

As he gathered so efficiently Chantal was left with time to stand and stare, but though the view from their mountain perch was magnificent her eyes were drawn more and more towards the supple, lean frame as the Marquis worked his way through the vineyard with a pantherish, half-crouched tread reminiscent of a jungle beast.

As the thought struck her she shivered. Was she being foolish in allowing this predator access to their territory? A monkey could be cunning, yet invariably he fell foul of the jungle hierarchy. Would that be her fate? Had she, in her unthinking eagerness, paved the way towards her own destruction?

'Are you cold?'

She jerked with surprise. He had seemed so absorbed in his work, yet her shiver had not escaped his alert, ever-searching eyes. He glanced at a watch strapped on to his brown wrist. 'What arrangements have you made for lunch? It's past midday, time we restoked our boilers,' he grinned.

As if the thought had been communicated by telepathy, Peter and Louis appeared in the distance. 'I'm famished, Sis!' Peter yelled when he was within hearing distance. 'I'll fetch the hamper! What about you, Brut, will you stay and share our lunch?'

The Marquis accepted with alacrity and did justice to the home-made soup, crusty bread and thick, tasty sausages Hortense had cooked the evening before. For dessert she had supplied crisp green apples. As the men sat back, replete, and had their cups replenished with wine they began, inevitably, to talk shop. The Marquis's first question took them by surprise, containing as it did an acceptance of their permanent residence in the district.

With his back propped against a tree, his long legs stretched out in front of him, he eyed the neat rows of vines, then lazily enquired of Peter, 'Have you considered any form of modernisation?—I am thinking along the lines of a more up-to-date method of spraying, a vital chore that has to be carried out a minimum of seven times between the months of May and August if pests and diseases are to be controlled. This vineyard is almost a quarter of a mile away from the nearest water supply, which means that Louis has to lug a wheelbarrow holding a barrel containing gallons of water along bumpy paths and up steep inclines, then retrace his steps to refill the barrel umpteen times in the course of one day. It says much for his powers of endurance that he has carried out the back-breaking job during the full heat of summer without so much as a murmur. Your grandmother and I had many arguments about this, but she could be extremely stubborn,' for some reason Chantal blushed when his glance fell upon her, 'and though very wealthy, was parsimonious in many small ways.'

'What improvements do you suggest we carry out?' Peter leant forward, his face alive with interest.

'The ideal solution for a small vineyard such as this,' the Marquis considered thoughtfully, 'would be to erect a water tank from which water could be pumped through pipes to a tap, or taps, positioned strategically within the vineyard.'

When Louis nodded enthusiastically Chantal felt

it was time to introduce a note of reality into the conversation before false hopes were further raised.

'There is the matter of finance to be considered, monsieur,' she rebuked with a frown. 'We would gladly do as you suggest if we had sufficient capital available—however, such a scheme is out of the question at the present moment.'

'The House would willingly advance the comparatively small sum needed to carry out such work.'

'No, thank you, monsieur,' she refused stiffly, very alive to the threat of allowing the Etablissement a financial hold over them. 'We will continue as we are for now, then as soon as we are able, once there is sufficient money to spare, we will certainly reconsider.'

'You may bitterly regret turning down my offer, Chantal.' Though the Marquis's tone was lazy her sensitive ears detected tiny splinters of steel. 'Ask Louis, here, how he feels when, after spending all day in roasting heat spraying the vines, returning home with eyes watering and burning, covered from head to foot in solution, he has to watch his day's labour being obliterated in minutes by an unexpected thunderstorm. The frustration is enough to make a strong man weep—he would weep less easily, feel less weary when beginning the job all over again, if there were tapped water near to hand.'

'I think we should accept——' Peter began eagerly.

'The Marquis probably has a point,' Chantal interrupted, determined not to be swayed, 'and it's very good of him to take such interest in our affairs. Nevertheless, for the reason I've already outlined, we must refuse his offer.'

'For heaven's sake, why ...?' Peter stormed, incensed by her stubbornness.

'Because I prefer hard work to debt,' she rebuked acidly. 'Labour can be painful, but so far as I'm concerned it's infinitely preferable to the agony of being under obligations.'

'We are nearer loving those who hate us than those who owe us more than we wish, eh?' Softly the Marquis quoted the maxim of La Rochefoucauld.

Amazed by his insight, Chantal's head swung towards him so that green eyes clashed with brilliant blue. 'Thank you for your understanding, monsieur, and please believe that my refusal isn't meant to be a snub.'

'Prove it!' Once again the lazy drawl became evident. 'Prove it by dropping that ridiculously formal mode of address and begin calling me Brut.'

It was such a short, abrupt little word, yet it stuck like a boulder in her throat. Twice she made an attempt while three pairs of amused eyes regarded her, enjoying her embarrassment, then finally it popped like a cork from a bottle, a sharp, loud release of pressure.

'Very well ... *Brut!*'

With cheeks afire she endured their laughter, but then, as if he had not inflicted embarrassment enough, her torturer continued to turn the screw. 'Well done, *ma belle châtaigne*, an heroic effort! Now, what about the function you and Peter have been invited to attend—won't you change your mind, help nurture the embryo of our friendship by promising me that you will come?'

Chantal had not intended to mention the affair to Peter because she had guessed what his reaction would be. After their small disagreement about Nicole he had been moodily subdued for a few days before his natural good humour was restored. But a fine hairline crack had developed in their affection, a crack she had no wish to see disturbed lest it should develop into a chasm. But that the Marquis's request had prised open the crack was made evident when Peter jumped to his feet to glare down at her, enraged.

'Since when have you taken it upon yourself to decide which invitations I ought to accept?' he challenged, his manly pride aroused. 'I'm no longer a child, to be patted on the head and told what's best for me, Sis, I'm a working man and as such can claim the right to a modicum of independence!' Swinging from her to the narrow-eyed Marquis, he informed him in a voice trembling with fury, 'Thank you for your invitation, Brut, on my own behalf, I accept with pleasure. In fact, you can tell Nicole that nothing will keep me away!'

CHAPTER SEVEN

LATER that evening, once dinner was over, Chantal broke Peter's moody silence by demanding a reply to her question.

'Would you mind telling me what you intend wearing at the do at the Château? Your school blazer, perhaps,' she could not resist a stab of sarcasm, 'or have you decided to impress the élite of Champenois society by turning up in a windbreaker and jeans?'

His horrified stare caused her a twinge of compunction. 'Glory ...! The question of what clothes to wear never crossed my mind! What the devil am I to do ...?'

Hortense chuckled. She seemed more and more to be enjoying these get-togethers around the dinner table, the laughter, the banter, the wrangling, the close circle of family intimacy inside which her beloved Louis was always included. It was questionable whether, as he sat toying with his cutlery, Louis had followed the conversation closely, so his short laugh could have been the result of genuine amusement or might simply have been an echo of his mother's. Whichever was the case, Peter took exception to it, venting his resentment with typical Champenois venom upon his victim's defenceless head.

'Laugh away, simpleton, fortunate twit that you

are, immune within your simple world from the smarts and hurts of normal people!'

Silence fell across the table—the silence of hurt from Louis, the silence of pain from Hortense, and from Chantal the silence of disgust and dismay. When eventually she found her voice its shocked, quivering timbre emphasised her anger. 'How dare you speak like that to a man who's gone to endless trouble to please you! Louis, with his generous heart, may find himself able to forgive your ill-mannered ignorance, but,' her voice cracked, 'I doubt if *I* ever shall!'

After Peter had flung out of the room, shame-faced yet defiant, she, Louis and Hortense consoled each other in silence, *compagnons misérables*, each wrapped in thought, each nursing an individual hurt. Finally, when the heavy ticking of a wall clock began to irritate, Chantal stirred herself sufficiently to ask,

'What's to be done with him, Hortense? Each year I expect more and more signs of maturity, but all that happens is that his tantrums grow worse, the arguments become less and less bearable.'

'Don't be too hard on him, *chérie*,' Hortense soothed, displaying surprising generosity. 'Youth possesses few faults that cannot be corrected with age. He is strong yet weak; mad yet sane; certain yet so lost. And to make matters even more complicated he thinks he is in love.'

'Infatuated, you mean.' Chantal frowned. 'Nicole is more than half to blame for turning his head, though why she should bother I simply can't understand. I'm convinced she has as little interest in the boy as her cousin has in me, yet both of them seem determined to assault us with their charm.'

'Could it be a case of tit for tat, do you suppose?' Hortense suggested dryly.

'I don't understand . . .' Chantal faltered.

'Well, I am merely trying to remind you that the man whom your mother jilted was both the Marquis's father and Nicole's uncle. Madame Mortemart, the mother of Nicole, still smarts from her brother's humiliation.'

Suddenly the burden on Chantal's shoulders seemed to grow even heavier. 'I'm beginning to realise how wrong we were to come here,' she admitted sadly.

Hortense became brisk. 'May I offer a suggestion, mademoiselle?'

'Please do,' she pleaded wearily.

'We are not too many miles away from a large town that is sure to contain one shop that supplies suits on hire for special occasions. If you could make your way there, taking with you your brother's measurements, I am sure you will manage to obtain an evening suit good enough to restore his humour.'

'You consider he deserves to be humoured?' Chantal's tone was dry.

'As a worker deserves his wages,' Hortense nodded. 'The boy has done well these past weeks, but the worst is yet to come. A small reward now might have the effect of rendering future chores a pleasure.'

After dwelling carefully on Hortense's words, Chantal decided that her advice was worth taking, so for the next few days she made various excuses to absent herself from the vineyard for an hour at a time in order to familiarise herself with the workings of the car, driving it round and round the courtyard until changing gear became less of an effort and she could reach without fumbling for every switch on the dashboard.

With the aid of a map supplied by Hortense she planned her route, opting to travel on as many secondary roads as possible in order to avoid heavy traffic and the hazards of roundabouts that she would have needed to negotiate by driving in a manner opposite to that to which she was familiar. The thought of having to drive along even quiet country lanes on the 'wrong' side of the road was daunting enough, so that when the day she decided to make her trip to town finally did arrive she set off with a dry mouth and a body tense to the fingertips.

The car showed its antiquity by creaking and groaning down the narrow road that sloped down the mountainside. Praying that no other vehicle would approach from the opposite direction, Chantal struggled against the effects of an awkward camber, keeping her eyes peeled for oncoming traffic, alive to the danger of some complacent speed-mad local hurtling around one of the many blind corners and bends. Mercifully, she gained the lower slopes without incident and turned on to the first level stretch of road marked on her map feeling a little more relaxed, gaining confidence enough to begin depressing the accelerator so that the car whizzed along the road stretching straight and empty for mile after mile.

She was humming softly beneath her breath, scoffing at her own earlier fears, when the car coughed, spluttered, then after a series of undignified jerks hiccoughed to a standstill. The smile melted from her lips as she clambered from the car and stood anxiously surveying the solitude she had cherished but that had now assumed a threatening aspect. No sign of life was evident, not even the roof of a cottage disturbed the green symmetry of trees and fields lining a road ribboning towards the horizon.

She shivered and scrambled back into the car when a gust of wind tugged the hem of her finely pleated skirt. The unexpected excitement of a trip to town had seemed to call for the wearing of her best outfit, a brown skirt and jacket of fine wool purchased months earlier in a fit of extravagance and worn only once at the wedding of a friend. With hindsight, she realised that a sweater would have been far more appropriate for a cold April day, but the yellow silk blouse, the colour of creamy butter, complemented the suit so well that in the comfort of a bedroom warmed by spring sunshine streaming through the windowpanes she had allowed vanity to overrule common sense.

'Well, you're suffering for it now, my girl!' she muttered through chattering teeth as she sat rubbing her arms to instil warmth, trying to decide whether it would be wiser to set off down the road in search of help or to remain where she was in the hope of a passing motorist offering a lift. Pessimistically, she glanced in the rear view mirror and felt a surge of thankfulness at the sight of a swiftly approaching car. Terrified that it might go speeding past, she jumped out of the car and stood in the middle of the road waving frantically. The car was within a few yards of her when realisation struck. Immediately, her arms slumped to her sides, the iced blood in her veins melted by a hot, embarrassed blush.

The car that drew to a smooth, silent standstill was as disdainfully aristocratic, as immediately recognisable as its owner, who greeted her with obvious annoyance.

'Never have I encountered a more foolhardy person than yourself! The chances you take,' the Marquis exploded, 'your reckless disregard of risk!' He seemed prepared to continue his scolding indefinitely, but when wind gusted, seemingly intent upon tearing the clothes from her body, he grabbed her by the elbow and pushed her towards his car.

'Get in,' he ordered tersely.

'But what about my car?' she began to protest.

'I will arrange for it to be towed into a garage and thoroughly serviced—as it ought to have been before you took it out on to the road,' he snapped. 'Have you no more sense than to attempt to drive a car that has stood for months without so much as an occasional warm-up to keep the engine ticking over? I had imagined that even Louis, simpleminded though he is, would have prevented such idiocy.'

'Please don't blame Louis,' she quickly protested, 'he had no inkling of my intention. Even now, he and Peter are unaware of the real reason behind my absence from the vineyard. The reason for my visit to town is to be a surprise for Peter, so it had to be kept secret.'

'I am aware of your plans,' he said, no whit mollified. 'When I called in at the house to be told that you had gone off for the day it did not take me long to discover the whys and wherefores from Hortense. I'm sorry my invitation has caused you problems, nevertheless there was no need for such a display of foolhardy independence—you must surely have known,' he grated, 'that I would have been willing at any time to give you a lift into town. *Lé bon dieu* was merciful. Just a few miles from here you would have been forced to join a main road that is part of a direct route from Paris to the Rhine basin—if the car had not broken down when it did, I have no doubt that I would have discovered you, and it, flattened beneath the wheels of some juggernaut!'

Downcast lashes flew up over eyes startled by the strangled savagery of his accusation, then widened further when for the first time she noted the tight line of his mouth, the pallor of cheeks showing white beneath his tan. Was he play-acting? she puzzled. If so, it was being superbly done. Then shamed by the suspicion, she decided that it would cost her nothing to give him the benefit of the doubt.

'I'm sorry to have put you to so much trouble,' she whispered.

'Sorry enough to make amends by allowing me to escort you into town?' he pounced with such lightning change of mood her suspicions immediately returned. Yet without his help she could find herself wandering the streets of a strange town, searching in vain for the shop she wanted. Her mission had to be accomplished in one day, no further time could be spared. Reluctantly, she had to accept his offer.

'You're very kind, monsieur, I shall be glad of your company.'

'*Brut* ...' He leant forward to switch on the ignition.

'Very well ... Brut,' she blurted, then sank into a painfully awkward silence.

Circumstances forced him to allow her this respite when not long afterwards they joined a road teeming with traffic of appalling density, lorries, coaches, cars and the inevitable juggernauts being driven at such speed and in some cases so erratically she knew that had she become embroiled within the tangle the conclusion Brut had drawn would have been inevitable. The thought was sobering, so much so that when eventually he branched off on to a road from which she could see buildings denoting the outskirts of a town, his glance across her pale features detected the sobering effect of narrowly-averted disaster.

'Shocking, was it not?' he queried lightly.

'You French people are mad!' she burst out, finding relief in anger. 'I've never experienced such atrocious driving!'

He shrugged. 'A man's true character is said to be revealed by the nature of his driving. While, in fairness to my countrymen, I must refute your charge of insanity, I must be equally fair and admit that a Frenchman exercises the same emotions when he is driving as he does when he is making love— he is impatient, he is reckless, and above all he is passionately desirous of achieving his goal.'

Chantal closed her eyes to block out the picture his words had formed, but quickly opened them again when the image immediately strengthened. His presence was torment enough without having to endure the added aggravation of carrying about in her mind a vision of what it would be like to be loved by a man Gallic to his very fingertips.

Surprise overcame embarrassment when they entered a thriving, bustling town full of large shops, fashionable cafés, theatres, cinemas and many office blocks advertising the headquarters of a dozen famous champagne firms. Brut drove to the rear of a building bearing the sign *Etablissement La Roque à Remi* and into a private car park marked into sections, each indicating the designation of the person for whom it was intended. When smoothly the bonnet of the car came to rest beneath a sign printed *Chef de Cave*, Chantal indicated it with a nod and queried diffidently:

'Won't he mind?'

'No, I do not mind in the least,' he laughed, easing long legs out of the car.

By the time he had walked around the rear and appeared at the side of the car to help her out his meaning had become clear.

'You are the Chef de Cave,' she accused, 'the man around whom the whole of the firm revolves! Yet you allowed me to think that you never actually *worked!*'

'You have formed so many preconceived ideas about me, *ma belle châtaigne*, that I am being forced to work methodically to eradicate them one by one.

My first task was to rid you of the false impression that I wished to see your brother and yourself fail in your courageous venture. My second was to prove that I am not the surly brute I must at first have appeared. And now,' he smiled, cupping her elbow in his hand to assist her to alight, 'I should like, if you will permit me, to atone for past indiscretions by ensuring that you enjoy this short break from your labours. It would help,' he urged softly, his blue eyes tracing the contours of her troubled face, 'if for a few hours you could lay suspicion aside and relax as if in the company of a friend.'

He really was the most plausible rogue, she told herself as, with her hand tucked within the crook of his arm, she was hustled through a confusion of side streets towards an outfitters that supplied suits for hire.

Within the space of fifteen minutes her business had been transacted and they left the shop with the promise that the goods they had chosen would be parcelled, ready to be picked up when later they returned.

'Lunch next, I think . . .' He glanced at his watch. 'There is an excellent hotel not far from here.'

'Oh, but . . .' Disappointment clouded her face.'

He halted. 'Please, don't make the excuse that you are not hungry! You English care so little for your stomachs—which is probably why your cooks omit loving care from the preparation of meals and rarely achieve succulence and sublety in sauces and garnishing.'

'No need to continue with the lecture,' she laughingly protested, 'I assure you that I'm hungry and

I do enjoy my food, it's simply that, if you have no objection, I would love to eat in a bistro.'

It must have been many years, if ever, since the aristocratic Marquis had entered such a workaday establishment, yet without hesitation he fell in with her wishes.

'*Certainement!* We will look for a place that is well filled with local people; what we are served may not be the best food in France, but still it will be very good indeed. The majority of my race are far more interested in what is on the plate than in the smartness of the surroundings.'

As it was comparatively early it did not take long to discover a place that promised to meet with his requirements. A delicious aroma met them as they stepped inside a warm, bustling, conversation-filled interior. A smiling *patronne* escorted them to one of the few empty tables and flicked an imaginary crumb from the spread of spotless chequered table-cloth, before offering proudly.

'May I recommend our dish of the day—*Salade aux moules à la Boulonnaise*?' She blew a rapturous kiss into the air. 'One of our chef's specialities!'

'Yes, please,' Chantal nodded, eager to try the dish she knew was a delicious mussel and potato salad.

'And no doubt Monsieur would like a carafe of wine?' the *patronne* enquired of the Marquis.

Chantal smiled to herself when, looking slightly pained, he communicated consent with a brief nod.

'Such places cannot as a rule offer an extensive wine list,' he complained, 'a bottle of *vin ordinaire* would be no more palatable than the local wines supplied by the carafe.'

'You're obviously spoiled,' she scolded with a smile, 'or perhaps your job has turned you into a wine snob.'

His eyebrows rose in response to her censure. 'On the contrary, a wine snob uses an imagined knowledge of wine to make unfortunate acquaintances feel inferior, whereas I have become embroiled over the years in a passionate love affair that has provided me with many mistresses. Each vintage, like every woman, has its own brand of seduction—a smell, a taste, a body so distinct that a man can close his eyes, sip, and identify immediately the blend of opulence and pleasure he is sampling.'

Chantal shifted uncomfortably, embarrassed by his choice of simile, but determined that her flippancy should be thoroughly punished, he continued to shock.

'From the cool, blonde German Hock he is given a reminder of an invigorating shower taken after toiling through the heat of a summer's day. In the company of a sweet, dark Spanish Oloroso he can relive the somnolent delight of basking under hot sun. From the cheerful Italian Chianti he receives the vitality of youth and the gluttonous enjoyment of eating a delicious meal. But only from Champagne,' he glinted wickedly, '*The maîtresse irrésistible*, can be gained an erotic pleasure similar to that of drinking wine from a French girl's navel.'

She was perfectly well aware that he was mocking her innate modesty and hated him for the satisfaction he displayed when, in spite of brave efforts to prevent it, a tide of colour rose swiftly to her cheeks.

To her relief his attention was diverted by the arrival of their meal, a large oval serving dish lined with potato slices, topped with mussels cooked in wine and a sprinkling of chopped parsley and chives, the whole sumptuously produced, skilfully prepared, and chilled to perfection.

To Chantal's untrained palate the rough peasant wine seemed to blend perfectly with the main course and also with the cheese she dared to select in preference to a sweet dessert, young goat's cheese, swaddled in bands of brown chestnut leaves which she slowly unwound to reveal a soft succulent centre dripping with moisture.

'I buy it from the gypsies, mademoiselle.' The *patronne* waited anxiously for her reaction. 'They deliver it to me fresh every day.'

'Mmm ... gorgeous!' Chantal mumbled, her mouth rather full.

The *patronne* beamed at the Marquis. 'It is most unusual for an English person to show appreciation of good food, monsieur.'

'Like the Eiswein, madame, the lady is indeed a rarity,' he agreed.

'Eiswein ...?' Chantal puzzled, her eyes wide with curiosity as she peeped across the rim of her glass.

'The famous German Ice Wine,' he exclaimed. 'When a late dry summer is followed by a quick hard frost the juice in the grapes becomes frozen. The grapes are then gathered and pressed when the juice is still frozen, the resultant wine being absolutely superb. The fact that the necessary climatic conditions occur very infrequently is responsible for the rarity of the wine, and explains why there have been only ten vintages of Eiswein in the last hundred years.'

'It seems to me that you place the highest value upon things that are not too readily available,' she decided slowly. 'Like a small boy, you desire most what you've been told you can't have.'

He shrugged. 'What we obtain too cheaply, we esteem too lightly. It is rarity that gives everything its value.'

Made bold by too much wine, Chantal flirted dangerously, green eyes sparkling a challenge across the safe width of the table. 'I'm flattered to be placed in the same category as a much sought-after vintage, but I find it a little disappointing that you made no mention of this wine among your list of ... er ... mistresses. Does the omission imply that I ... that *it* lacks some quality essential to your pleasure?'

His smooth reply stripped the conversation of all pretence that they were speaking exclusively on the subject of wine.

'Indeed not.' His assessing smile caused her a sobering pang. 'The object of learning about wine is not just to achieve sufficient knowledge to appreciate those wines that have become established favourites, but also to supply guidelines to those who wish to explore the possibilities of any delightful new discoveries. A man's taste can become jaded, familiarity breeds boredom, so he begins looking elsewhere in search of fresh interests to titillate his senses.' The words rolled from his tongue in the manner of a *chef de cave* following the routine of his profession, thoroughly tasting, analysing, and then discarding.

'*Here,*' Chantal heard an inner voice of caution, '*is a man who will discard women as often, and with as little thought, as he would discard an inferior wine.*' Only a superwoman could hope to achieve the standard of perfection he demanded—only a superwoman could cope with the pain of being rejected if she did not!

She was quiet during the return journey, and as Brut too, seemed occupied with thoughts of his own, the drive was accomplished practically in silence. There was no reason that she could think of for the sudden bout of depression that had dropped like a cloud over what had turned out to be a very enjoyable day. Not a relaxing one by any means; it was impossible to relax in the company of a man who loved to torment, which was probably why she felt so tired, why she could be grateful for the fact that because his mood matched hers she was being spared the effort of searching for flippant replies to his usually teasing comments.

She chanced a sideways glance and saw that his aquiline features were stern, almost morose, as he divided his attention between his driving and the thoughts that had chased devilment from his eyes and the curled, slightly derisive smile from his lips. It would be so easy to become charmed by him, she thought, a breath catching sharply in her throat. It was useless trying to deny that she found him intensely attractive, or that with a quirk of an eyebrow, an unexpected smile, he could stampede her immature senses. Yet innate common sense warned her that the attraction was purely physical, and besides that, deliberately contrived. Which was why she had to remain always on the defensive, remembering always that she was participating in what might turn out to be a very dangerous game!

With her armour of self-confidence renewed, she was able to turn upon him a cool, enquiring look when just as they came within sight of Trésor d'Hélène he pulled into the side of the road, switched off the ignition, then twisted in his seat to face her. When, without a word, he snaked an arm across the back of her seat to grip her shoulder she tensed. She just had time to register: 'Oh, God, he's so predictable ...!' before he lowered his head and captured her mouth beneath his in a long, draining kiss.

Scorn offered little immunity to the shattering impact upon her senses as his mouth searched and probed, arousing deeply buried nerves into quivering life, setting a torch to emotions that had lain tidy, neat and untouched waiting for a flame to leap them into fiery life. When finally he withdrew his lips from hers she felt she had been consumed, as fire consumes everything before it, leaving her heart, her senses, her emotions no more than a litter of charred debris.

Only her eyes remained alive in an ashen face, darkly green, turbulent with anger and contempt. With breath escaping from her lips in strangled gasps, she managed to hiss!

'I trust that the payment you've extracted was sufficient, monsieur?'

Furiously, she wrenched open the door, then

changed her mind and twisted round to face him.

'Just in case it wasn't, I'd better leave a tip!'

The sound of her palm connecting against his cheek was music in her ears after she jumped from the car and ran from the man who had made no attempt to fend off her blow, who had not flinched, not even when the signet ring on her finger had cut deeply into his lip.

CHAPTER EIGHT

'MADEMOISELLE, have you decided what *you* are going to wear to the ball at the Château?' Hortense was checking through the contents of the linen cupboard and Chantal, because she was not needed that day in the vineyard, was helping her.

Angry because her hands had suddenly begun to shake, she thrust them inside the pockets of her skirt and replied moodily,

'Peter will have to go alone, I have nothing suitable in my wardrobe for such a posh affair and it would be a sinful waste of money to buy an extravagant dress for one night only. No, Peter must convey my apologies, I'm certain he won't mind going alone.'

'I'm quite sure he will not,' Hortense hesitated as if searching for words, 'but are you sure it would be wise to allow him to do so? The boy's attitude has changed for the better since you found a suit for him to wear. His apology to Louis was sincere and they are once more the best of friends. He has done me many small kindnesses in order to atone, and I know that the relationship between the two of you has been restored almost to normal. And yet ...'

'I know what you're going to say,' Chantal sighed. 'There's an air of suppressed excitement about him that's very worrying. He's been with Nicole for some part of every day since she returned from Paris two weeks ago. He hasn't shirked his share of the work, but I can't see how the presence of Nicole in the vineyard, trailing in his shadow, flirting prettily while pretending to help, can have been anything other than a hindrance. I've given her no encouragement, indeed, on one or two occasions I've been on the verge of delivering a definite snub, but because I don't want to anger Peter further I've managed to bite my tongue. What's her aim, Hortense?' she burst out anxiously. 'The two of them are much of an age, but compared with Nicole my brother is as sophisticated as a babe in arms!'

'I have no idea, mademoiselle,' Hortense shook her head, 'but this much I do know—Nicole has inherited her mother's devious ways. I would not trust either of them an inch, which is why I am urging you to attend the ball if only to keep an eye on your brother! I fear Nicole is playing with his emotions as a cat would play with a mouse; soon she will tire of the novelty and as a consequence he will be very hurt. As it is useless trying to reason with him, I think you should stay close by his side in case help should be needed.'

'But I *can't* go to the ball!' wailed Chantal. 'As I've already explained, I can't afford to buy a new dress.'

'Then we will make one,' Hortense insisted. 'There are three whole days left before the ball is to be held.'

'Make one?' Chantal stared. 'How? I have no material, and even if I had who do we know who's clever enough to run up a dress suitable for such an occasion?'

Hortense bridled. Slightly offended, she exclaimed, 'You see before you, mademoiselle, one who has spent the better part of her life as a lady's maid. Part of my duties was to cut out and sew dresses for far grander occasions than the one we are discussing—and what is more,' she sniffed, 'if my work was good enough to satisfy your grandmother who, as everyone knows, set extremely high standards, I see no reason why it should not be equally satisfactory to you.'

Chantal had resigned herself to staying away from the ball, but only now, when a faint hope of going had presented itself, did she realise how much she was missing the company of others outside of their small tight circle. It would be fun to forget work for one day at least, to dress up and feel young and carefree again, to dance, perhaps ...

She shied away from picturing herself in the arms of one particular man and asked anxiously of Hortense, 'Do you really think it possible? Could we get the material in time?'

Hortense preened. 'There is a wealth of material upstairs in the attic, dozens of trunks containing dresses that belonged to your grandmother, all carefully wrapped to preserve the material. Among them we are sure to find one that could be restyled or unpicked, perhaps, so that the material can be fashioned into a dress of your own design. If you could perhaps sketch out a design for me to copy ... ?'

'I certainly can, Hortense, you clever, clever dear!' Chantal enveloped the old woman in a warm hug. 'Come on, let's see what we can find!'

Hortense had not exaggerated. The attic, which Chantal had not previously visited, was lined with trunks packed with every dress the Comtesse had owned from the day of her marriage until a few years previous to her death. There were skirts of lightweight tweed, immaculate as the day the cloth had been woven; blouses of cotton and shimmering silk; day gowns; cocktail dresses and evening wear in every colour, style and material imaginable. She pounced upon every article, preening in front of a fly-blown mirror as she posed with each dress held up in front of her. But by the time an enjoyable hour had passed they had to call a halt, confused by the colourful profusion of silks, brocades, chiffons and laces piled knee-deep around them.

'Did my grandmother never throw *anything* away?' Chantal gasped, sinking wide-eyed on to a nearby trunk.

'Never.' Hortense blinked, misty-eyed with the revival of many memories. 'She could be generous to a fault, and yet in many little ways she showed a thriftiness typical of all French women. If ever she saw a poor woman in need of a coat she would buy her one, yet she was loath to part with any of her own possessions—especially clothes that she had worn on happy occasions. This dress, for instance,' she held up a gown of dark brown velvet with a bodice inset with lace and a high, boned collar, 'was one of her special favourites. She wore it often, especially,' the old woman chuckled, 'when she wished to wheedle some extra favour from your grandfather—even though she was perfectly well aware that whichever dress she happened to be wearing he would still find her irresistible.'

Tentatively, because in the past Hortense had always been reticent on the subject of her late mistress, Chantal asked:

'Was she very lovely?'

'Lovely?' Hortense's expression dismissed the adjective as inadequate. 'She was the most beautiful, the most frivolous, the most extravagant, the most coquettish, the most outstanding of all her generation of Champagne Girls. Her father spoiled and adored her. Unlike Monsieur le Marquis, who is a cultured, highly intelligent *grand seigneur*, the Comtesse's father, who was a co-founder of the firm La Roque à Remi, was more at home in his vineyards than in his office, loved the country much more than the town, and yet he managed to make a fortune large enough to provide his only daughter with a *dot* sufficiently large to attract a husband from the ranks of the titled aristocracy. Yes,' she nodded sagely, 'Monsieur le Comte d'Estrées must have counted himself a very fortunate man on his wedding day.'

'Do you mean,' Chantal almost choked on her indignation, 'that he married her only for gain? That had her *dot* not been large enough he would have passed her over in favour of a richer bride?'

'*Mais certainement.*' Hortense seemed puzzled by her fury. 'It is the custom in our country that every girl who desires to become a bride must have a *dot*. Not only must she be well provided for in the matter of outfits, clothes and linen, but if she cannot offer in addition a substantial sum of money according to the position of the man she wishes to marry she cannot hope to take him as a husband! I pro-

vided my own *dot*,' she concluded proudly, 'and as
my parents were dead I had to work many extra
hours in order to swell my savings.'

'How despicable!' Disgust was written all over
Chantal's face. 'I couldn't stand being sized up,
priced, then bargained for like cattle at a market!
If a man couldn't love me for myself I'd say good
riddance!'

Hortense smiled, pitying her ignorance. 'Frenchmen have little or nothing to say in the matter of
marriage, mademoiselle, whether it is their own or
their son's. Negotiations are left entirely in the
hands of the womenfolk, for as everyone knows, we
are far more businesslike, more astute, keener in
judgment than any man and we therefore manage
to drive a harder bargain.'

'Doesn't anyone in your country ever marry for
love?' asked Chantal, scandalised.

'As for today, I cannot say,' Hortense shrugged,
'but in the old days it was very seldom the case. But
times have changed even in this quiet backwater.
Nevertheless,' she added thoughtfully, 'I heard only
recently of a man of ambition who, though attracted
to another, chose as his wife the daughter of a vineyard owner in order to ensure that eventually he
will acquire more land.'

Hortense rambled on, unaware that her stunned,
incredulous listener had become deaf to her words.

*'I heard only recently of a man of ambition who,
though attracted to another, chose as his wife the
daughter of a vineyard owner in order to ensure that
eventually he will acquire more land.'*

The words were pounding in Chantal's ears, hammering home a message of greed and cold, calculated deceit. *Could* Hortense have unknowingly supplied the answer to the riddle that had been puzzling her? Did the Champenois still cling with such tenacity and insistence to outdated marriage customs that even today the Marquis and Nicole were prepared to enter cold-bloodedly into a marriage without love if in exchange they gained a coveted piece of land? Dazedly, she shook her head, attempting to disperse the impossible thought. Surely not even the Marquis and his cousin—Champenois to the core though they might be—would go to such lengths to restore Trésor d'Hélène to the Etablissement La Roque à Remi!

Though her enthusiasm had waned, Chantal could not help but be impressed when Hortense delved into the last of the chests and emerged uttering a triumphant exclamation.

'*Très magnifique!* Look, mademoiselle, can you not picture yourself wearing this!'

Chantal looked up, her eyes still troubled, and caught her breath in a gasp of admiration when Hortense spread wide the skirt of a crinoline ball dress, layers and layers of crisp green net, ruffles, and rustling petticoats. It was a dress straight out of the archives of a romantic era, an echo from the age of horse-drawn carriages, candlelit dining-rooms and a rich, pampered society whose daughters had had all the time in the world to prepare the elaborate toilette such a dress demanded.

'Oh, I couldn't wear that, Hortense!' Her first reaction was one of panic. 'It's beautiful, but far too grand for me.'

Hortense tut-tutted. 'Every girl should wear a dress like this at least once in her lifetime, mademoiselle! We all need a little romance, something to dream about when we are older, but,' she sighed, allowing the dress to drop from her hands, 'perhaps it is a little old-fashioned.'

'Actually,' Chantal told her thoughtfully, 'it's anything but. According to the fashion magazine I was reading during my journey here, all the top fashion houses are tuning in to the current demand for dressier, more feminine clothes. One designer in particular, it was reported, chanced half a dozen crinolines in his last collection and was amazed when they easily outsold everything else in his range. So you see, it's not just the wearing of the dress that worries me, it's all the bits and pieces that go with it—expertly coiffured hair, immaculate nails, terrific make-up, gloves, the right jewellery ... Look at me, Hortense, and tell me truthfully, could I possibly do justice to such finery?'

She became slightly discomfited when Hortense took her at her word and began slowly and carefully to evaluate her assets. Casting over her the shrewd, experienced eyes of a woman who for years had dressed and attended a mistress whose chic elegance had been the envy of her contemporaries, she considered. Long, silent minutes passed before she proffered an opinion.

'You have all the attributes your grandmother possessed except one—the ability to flaunt them. She had the power to captivate men and did not hesitate to use it—if you did the same the result might surprise you.'

Chantal's response was a wry grimace. 'The fashion for wearing crinolines may have been revived, but the old-fashioned attitudes that went with them certainly have not. Today, women expect men to treat them as intelligent human beings, not just charming playthings.'

'So I have noticed,' Hortense snorted, 'and it is women who play down their femininity in order to be accepted into the fellowship of men who are the losers. Such women consider that to be called "feminine" is an insult and if they had their way they would eradicate the word "female" from every dictionary. But fortunately all women are not deceived by such nonsense, some are wise enough to cling to the aura of mystery that is woman's most powerful asset. The ability to entrance is nature's greatest gift to our sex. Tell me,' she demanded of Chantal, 'have you never wanted to be the centre of a man's universe? If you answer no to that question,' she went on quickly, 'then I pity you, for you have never been in love. If you wish to share in this wonderful, exciting experience that will never go out of fashion you must be prepared, as your grandmother always was, to make use of every magic quality, to be feminine, provocative, and above all, *accessible*!'

'Really, Hortense!' Chantal did not know whether to be amused or shocked by the old woman's vehemence. 'If I had to take your advice I'd feel little better than a huntress laying bait to trap an unwary male!'

'Precisely!' Hortense beamed. 'You are a quick pupil, mademoiselle. Men are lured by danger, they find it enormously fascinating—is it not fortunate that, where a woman lacks strength, she can compensate with the use of strategy?'

Strategy! Unknowingly, Hortense had chosen a word very appropriate to the circumstances—the art of war, the art of directing military movement so as to secure the most advantageous positions and combinations of forces. At the moment Chantal and Peter were placed in a most disadvantageous position, her brother was oblivious to danger, but she was very conscious of the fact that she was fighting with her back to the wall. If ever strategy was needed it was now. Her best ally, she mused, would be the element of surprise, a tactic the Marquis himself had used very successfully, therefore he could hardly complain if he was paid back in his own coin. The question was, did she possess sufficient ability? What use were weapons, however sharp, if they could not be handled with expertise?

She was, however, a born fighter. But it was courage born of ignorance that prompted her decision. 'Three days is barely long enough to improve my neglected appearance, but I intend to try, Hortense, that is, if you think you can have the dress ready in time?'

'I'm positive I can, mademoiselle,' Hortense beamed her delight. 'If the style is to your liking, then what alterations are needed will be minor, for at the time this dress was made your grandmother was similar to yourself in size.' Gathering up the cloud of tulle, she assured Chantal, 'Your hair will pose no problem, it looks to be in superb condition, glossy and bright as a ripe chestnut.'

Ma belle châtaigne. The Marquis's favourite description impinged against her newly-donned armour of confidence. My *beautiful chestnut* ... ! Chantal winced from the reminder and forced herself to pay attention to Hortense's excited babble of words.

'It is a great pity that your grandmother's jewellery has been disposed of, but there is one very important accessory still available. Perfume,' Hortense supplied in response to Chantal's raised eyebrows. 'Your grandmother was a great believer in perfume as an aid to success in every imaginable situation. So fascinated was she by its history that she read every book she could find on the subject, becoming so expert on its effects that eventually she compiled a chart explaining the type of impact one could expect from each of the various essences. Her magic potions, she called them, and they certainly seemed to work magic for her! Some women prefer to stick to one particular blend until it becomes as personal to them as their signature, but Madame la Comtesse preferred to experiment, choosing a different perfume to match each mood. Come,' she beckoned Chantal towards the stairs, 'let me show you.'

Doubtful whether a perfume had ever been created to match a mood of determined revenge, Chantal followed the housekeeper downstairs towards a small dressing-room where most of her grandmother's possessions were stored. Previously she had not been allowed entry, the door had remained locked, the jealously guarded key always in Hortense's possession, but as if in some way the short discourse about her grandmother had helped soften her attitude, Hortense unlocked the door, then stepped aside, indicating with a flourish that it was Chantal's right to enter first.

What furniture the room contained was shrouded in dustcovers. Throwing one of them aside to reveal a small cabinet, Hortense slid open a drawer and withdrew a lacquered box which she set down upon a table before lifting the lid. Inside the dark interior, fitted into individual slots, were many small phials of perfume, prominently labelled, their seals still intact.

'I threw out those bottles that had been opened; these that are left should have retained their original strength. See,' she pointed to the lid, 'there is the chart the Comtesse compiled!'

Curiously, Chantal lifted out several close-written pages of script and began to read.

'How can it be argued,' her grandmother questioned from the past, 'that scent is no more than an accessory when it is a well known fact that physical ills can be cured by massaging with essential oils and also that even primitive African tribes smear themselves with scent to protect themselves from evil spirits? I firmly believe that smells have the power to disarm an enemy, to weave spells, to annihilate opponents, and to create an aura of enchantment that is irresistible to men.'

Then, under a heading 'Aids to Seduction' were listed: Orange blossom—helpful in blunting the mind; used when wishing to slow down a man's reasoning faculties. Patchouli: useful whenever a stimulant is required. Jasmine: a nerve sedative to induce feelings of optimism and euphoria.

Many more essences were itemised under headings: To Sedate; to Comfort; to Uplift; to Stimulate; to Reassure, together with snippets of advice ranging from which essence to choose when wishing to project warmth and sympathy to those suitable for anyone needing to combat anger, irritability and downright rage.

'The most important thing to remember,' her forthright grandmother had concluded, 'is that man is a sentimentalist and anything that recalls fond memories will be instantly appreciated. Frenchmen, in particular, are especially susceptible to lily of the valley (fond memories of May 1st).'

Feeling she had been privileged to peep into the mind of a very humorous, very lovable lady, Chantal laid down the papers and enquired of Hortense:

'What's significant about the date May the first?'

When Hortense smiled she looked for an instant young again as her eyes reflected happy memories of long ago. 'On that day, in Paris, it is traditional that anyone who is handed a sprig of lily of the valley must give a kiss in return. The custom began many years ago when one day a young man walking through the woods near Paris picked a bouquet of lily of the valley to take to his sweetheart. He received a kiss in exchange. The day was the first of May, and so even to this very day, on May the first, anyone who is given this flower is expected to give a kiss in return. Even the authorities are kind, they have decreed that it is the one day of the year when lily of the valley can be sold from flower carts without a licence, so the streets are filled with its fragrance and with men and women, boys and girls, all exchanging kisses—also without licence. Have you not realised,' she questioned slyly, 'that May the first is also the date when the ball is due to be held at the Château? Perhaps there you will find a sweetheart—a husband, even—but if you should achieve neither, you will most certainly be called upon to forfeit many, many kisses!'

CHAPTER NINE

THE Château was floodlit. Set upon a gentle slope against a backcloth of dark trees the round towers, imposing chimneys and pyramid-topped pavilions seemed carved out of buttery stone. As they drove past a scalloped half-moat and entered a drive lined with ancient plane trees Chantal experienced panicky second thoughts. She had expected to be impressed by the Marquis's home, but not overwhelmed, this was no mere habitation, it was the establishment of a *grand seigneur*.

In other circumstances she would have stopped to admire the pair of elegant-necked swans majestically skimming the waters of a lake positioned directly opposite a flight of steps leading up to an entrance that had its doors thrown wide to welcome the stream of guests alighting with much laughter and excited conversation from cars lining nose to tail along the length of the drive.

They had not known that it was to be a *bal masqué* until the actual invitation arrived, a silver-scrolled request for their company together with, tucked inside the large envelope, two masks provided by their thoughtful host.

When Louis drove off, leaving them stranded at the foot of the steps, Chantal and Peter exchanged a nervous look. They both felt on edge, selfconscious in their unaccustomed finery, certain that within this gathering of aristocrats and local celebrities they would be bound to commit some horrible *gaffe*.

Suddenly reminded of his duties as an escort, Peter drew in a sharp breath and squared his shoulders. 'Come on, Sis,' he offered her an arm, 'there's no need for you to be nervous, you look terrific!'

She tried to smile at her young brother, who was looking unfamiliarly mature in an evening suit that made his figure look taller, his shoulders broader. His face was stern, his eyes, framed in a black silken mask, striving unsuccessfully not to twinkle. Aware that he was sharing her feeling of nervous fright, she forced a frivolous reply.

'You're looking pretty devastating yourself, young sir.' She dropped a mocking curtsey. 'It does my morale no end of good to have such a presentable male as an escort.'

'Stop fishing for compliments,' he chided with brotherly candour. 'For the past hour I've been telling you at regular ten-minute intervals how stunning you look, and with equal regularity you've replied in kind. We'll get nowhere standing here exchanging compliments, so, as our egos have been sufficiently boosted, let's go inside.'

As slowly they ascended the steps towards a spill of laughter, lights and music Chantal felt confidence seeping at every step. Frantically, as the large open doorway drew nearer she tried to bolster her spirits by recalling the reactions of her companions when she had appeared downstairs to join them for an aperitif before setting off for the Château. She had known that she was looking her best, her own efforts of the past three days, together with the results achieved by Hortense's skilful needlework, had paid off, so much so that as she had stolen a last exultant peep in the mirror her spirits had soared. Even so, the response from the others had been gratifying.

'*Ma belle enfant!*' Hortense had cried. 'You look *ravissante!*' Laughingly, Chantal had twirled in front of Louis inviting comment. As the green froth of tulle, net and tiers of rustling petticoats had billowed around her ankles his doe-soft eyes had devoured burnished hair swept high to expose an exquisite cameo profile, a smooth brow, high cheekbones curving softly downwards to a small pointed chin, and a trembling mouth the colour of the wild carnations he often gathered from secret sunny places in the height of summer. Her misty eyes reminded him of green grapes veiled by fine bloom. Slowly his eyes had shifted downwards to rest upon creamy shoulders rising from a diaphanous green cloud, then quickly he had looked away, blushing, as his simple mind wrestled with the awesome problems that could confront a girl wearing a dress with no visible means of support. He had no way of knowing that expediency was forcing her to suffer the rigours inescapable from the vanity of yesteryear.

'Whalebone supports are essential to the dress,' Hortense had insisted firmly when Chantal had suggested they might be removed, 'how else is one to achieve the tiny waist, the provocative swell of bosom?'

'Well, Louis, what's your opinion?' Chantal had

prompted, then had reacted with a catch of pleasure to his mumbled reply.

'*Vous êtes la plus belle fille du monde!*' You are the most beautiful girl in the world! He had hesitated, painfully searching for words, and had been rewarded by a flash of inspiration. 'You ... you smell like woods full of *muguet des bois* after a shower of rain!'

The swell of music grew louder and as light fell across her face Chantal hesitated, clutching Peter's arm as he was about to guide her across the threshold.

'Is my mask straight?' she quavered, touching nervous fingers to the decorative silver strip shading her eyes.

'It's fine,' he encouraged gently. 'Don't be afraid, everyone will be wearing one, so we'll all be strangers until twelve o'clock, at least.'

She had not thought of that. Bolstered by the knowledge, she once more accepted his arm and allowed him to sweep her inside.

In keeping with the informality of the occasion, no names were announced, no introductions were made. As they stepped inside a magnificent hall Chantal caught a glimpse of a great stairway spilling like a princess's train across the black and white marble floor, great wall mirrors, the glitter of ormolu, and an impression of wood, silk, and wool faded with age to shades of muted splendour.

A footman took their coats, a second accepted their invitation card and a third escorted them towards large double doors thrown wide open, then bowed, leaving them on the threshold of a *grand salon* huge enough to accommodate in comfort the hundreds of couples standing chatting in groups, sitting around tables, circulating from one company to another, and dancing to a hit tune of the moment being belted out by a group of musicians seated at the far end of the *salon*.

Immediately they stepped inside a young couple split up and claimed them as partners and before Chantal had time to feel nervous, or even to search for a glimpse of a blond, proudly-held head, she was swept into the middle of the dance floor by her wildly energetic partner.

Amazingly, within the informal atmosphere, and together with a succession of partners who saw to it that she did not sit out even one dance, she discovered that she was thoroughly enjoying the company of predominantly young men who, caught up in the enjoyment of mysterious anonymity engendered by concealing masks, insisted upon introducing themselves by their first names only. Once or twice she caught sight of Peter dancing past with a dark-haired girl in a startling red dress that could only have been Nicole, but not once during three hectic hours of merriment did she see the man who was uppermost in her mind, the man on whose behalf she had daubed herself with a liberal amount of muguet des bois, the scent to which, according to her grandmother, Frenchmen were especially susceptible.

Supper was provided from an elaborate buffet served from tables set out in a separate room. After being persuaded to try a helping of lobster, another of smoked sheep's tongues and a portion of *cremet*

—a superb mixture of cream and curd, sprinkled with sugar and served with tiny strawberries which she found so irresistible she could not refuse a second helping—tiredness began pressing heavily behind her eyes, making it difficult to stay awake.

'Too much champagne!' she scolded herself, hiding a yawn behind outspread fingers. The room seemed to have become oppressively hot, so, feeling more than a little lightheaded, she dodged the attention of her current escort and began edging out of the room in search of a quiet spot in which she might regain her composure, as well as a breath of reviving air.

Stumbling into a deserted hallway, she hesitated, undecided, wondering behind which of the many doors she would be safe. Cautiously, she advanced on tiptoe towards the nearest, depressed the handle, then stepped into a room that was a perfect oasis of peace and calm. Sparing barely a glance for huge candelabra, lanterns of gilded bronze, the framed portraits hung upon the walls, she sank down on to a high-backed, velvet-covered sofa, snuggled deep into the cushions, and with a sigh of satisfaction closed her eyes.

Barely half an hour had passed when she was awakened by a voice speaking her name. Before she could move, a second voice made a reply, a hard, brittle tone which she immediately recognised as Nicole's.

'Had I known you were anxious to make the acquaintance of Mademoiselle Barry and her brother I would have introduced them to you as soon as they arrived. But knowing how much you dislike these informal affairs, Maman, I assumed that you would wish to follow your usual custom of remaining out of sight for as long as is politely possible. However, now that you are ready to join the rest of the guests I will search them out for you.'

'I am not at all anxious to meet them, as you are very well aware, Nicole.' Without even seeing her Chantal guessed that Nicole's mother's expression was as acid as her voice. 'I merely wish to be kept informed of their intentions. What I cannot understand is why Brut insisted upon inviting them here, nor am I happy about the way you and he have fraternised with the Barrys ever since their arrival.'

'*Fraternised* ...!' Nicole's laughter was sharp. 'You speak of them as if they are dangerous enemies, Maman!'

'Well, aren't they ... ?'

Chantal crouched into a tense ball, praying that the two women would not move into the centre of the room to discover her skulking on the sofa.

'Enemies, perhaps,' Nicole agreed negligently, 'but dangerous? Never ... ! The boy especially is callow, awkward, and screamingly funny when he attempts to imitate his sophisticated elders. For weeks I have forced myself to endure his clumsy pawing, his moist, immature kisses, but my exercise in restraint is paying off and I can now mould him like putty in my hands.'

'But why?' her mother sniffed. 'For what purpose?'

Nicole's tongue clicked with aggravation. 'For the purpose of regaining what rightly belongs to the Etablissement, of course. I surely don't have to spell

out to you of all people how important the vineyards of Trésor d'Hélène are to the House? The
Barrys had no moral right to take over ownership,
if the Comtesse had not been so acquisitive, if she
had not hung on to the land too long, it would
naturally have been willed to Brut. It was as good as
stolen from him, so we intend to deprive the Barrys
of the land that ought never to have been theirs.'

'And how do you propose to do that?' Her mother
sounded contemptuously amused.

'By copying the ways of our ancestors,' Nicole addressed her mother in a tone of hard dislike. 'Didn't
my father acquire his vineyards by marrying you?
And haven't you many times stated that your
brother, Brut's father, was upset when his intended
eloped with her lieutenant not so much because he
had lost a bride but because he had lost all hope of
gaining the land he coveted?'

'You are cruel, Nicole!' her mother hissed, 'cruel
and selfish—too selfish to sacrifice your own happiness by marrying a callow youth!'

'Too true, Maman ... !' Nicole's trill of laughter
pierced the ice that had formed around Chantal's
heart. 'The only husband I want is Brut. But Peter
need not become acquainted with that fact until
after he has been persuaded to sign over his half of
Trésor d'Hélène to me. Once Brut has gained possession of the other half the outcome cannot be in
doubt. Even he, wary bachelor though he is, will be
forced to bow to the inevitable. I have no doubt
whatsoever that he will be eager to combine the two
halves—so ensuring a perfect marriage.'

'How outrageous!' Her mother did not sound

outraged, merely amused. 'Where is Brut, by the way? It is almost time for the unmasking.'

'He is tied up with local dignitaries—pompous bores who consider it beneath their dignity to mix with the younger element.' There was a rustle of skirts as the two women began moving towards the door. 'It is time that he, too, had a little fun; I'll go and rescue him with the reminder that it is his duty to distribute the flowers.'

When the door closed behind them Chantal remained seated, her fists tightly clenched, her limbs shaking as she fought to control shock, anger and horrified revulsion. The conversation she had overheard had told her nothing new, it had only clarified what she had already suspected, yet to have heard the plot outlined with such cold-blooded indifference to any hurt inflicted upon Peter and herself was to come face to face with a cruelty so barbaric it took her breath away. Robespierre could not have displayed less humanity when deciding which of his enemies were to be guillotined. And as for Nicole's mother, it was easy to imagine her as one of a crowd of gloating revolutionaries applauding with delight while heads rolled.

A shudder racked her out of her frozen trance.

Glancing at a clock upon the wall she saw that it was almost midnight, the moment of unmasking, the time when missing faces would cause comment! She stood up, stiffened by resolve, and moved without thinking to peer into a wall mirror. Amazingly, the face she saw reflected looked composed, a little white, a little pinched around mouth and nostrils, but the eyes deceivingly serene, giving no hint of the white-hot anger seething within.

'If the Marquis wants to play his dirty game then let him!' she fiercely advised her image as she smoothed an errant wisp of hair. 'Mere words won't convince Peter of their duplicity, but if you play the Marquis along pretending to fall in love with him,' she almost choked on the words, 'sooner or later he'll slip up, reveal his true colours, then Peter will be bound to be convinced.'

She flinched from examining too deeply the trauma that was sure to evolve from flirting dangerously with the devil. 'It *must* be done, if only for Peter's sake!' she scolded her suddenly whitened features. 'So pull yourself together and get in there *fighting*!'

She managed to sidle unnoticed into the salon just as the band reached a final crescendo and a signal was given to remove all masks. Edging around the fringe of laughing, excited merrymakers, she made towards an alcove where curtains were billowing across french windows left open to create a welcome draught of air. Her heart began to pound when she caught sight of the Marquis, smiling and debonair, standing beside a table laden with shallow wicker baskets filled with fragile, bell-shaped flowers, their white heads nodding against a background of dark green foliage. Blood drumming in her ears made her deaf to his words, but when after a loud cheer of approval all the men rushed forward to claim a spray of *muguet des bois*—their licence to love—it became obvious to Chantal that the time for kissing had begun.

Pulses rioted when, standing with her back

pressed against the wall, she saw the Marquis advancing towards her. Courage evaporated at the sight of the flowers he obviously meant to present in order to claim a rewarding kiss. With a gasp of sheer panic she twirled on her heel and escaped through a gap in the curtains on to a dark, deserted terrace.

Her flight was abortive, a mere challenge to the man who treasured above all else that which was not too easily attainable. She tried not to cower when his dark bulk towered over her. His face was in shadow, but the mockery in his voice was unmistakable when he bowed and presented his gift.

'For you, mademoiselle, I bring flowers of the woods, in the hope that I may be permitted to compare their pale fragrant beauty with the petal softness of your lips.'

Her low gasp of dissent was smothered when his forceful mouth captured hers in a kiss so vibrant it shocked alive every pulsating nerve. Helplessly she clung to him while he plundered her lips of sweetness, draining his fill, tenacious as a bee foraging into the heart of a flower.

Gradually she forced herself to surrender, delighting him with a response that was shy at first, then escalated with courageous boldness. Dredging her mind of every hint of seduction she had ever read, copying the actions of film stars she had seen acting out torrid love scenes, she pressed her body close to his, forced leaden arms around his neck and parted soft lips beneath his questing mouth, simulating the hungry desire of a woman utterly and totally captivated.

Predictably, he was surprised, the surprise of a

warrior with mind and body conditioned to engage in a long and weary battle only to discover his opponent falling at his feet at first encounter. Chantal's greatest ally in duplicity was the fact that a man gripped by intense arousal will believe anything he wants to believe, which was why her low moans of self-disgust were mistaken for gasps of pleasure, when his hands gripped close a body trembling with what he imagined to be uncontrollable passion but which, in reality, was acute revulsion.

Feeling the wetness of tears beneath his searching lips, he cradled her in his arms and rocked her gently, scolding in a hoarse murmur.

'Please don't cry, *mon ange*, with me you need never feel afraid ...'

She was not merely afraid, she was terrified, terrified that the hatred surging inside of her would erupt, overruling her determination not to give in to an urge to bite savagely into his lip, not to utilise the many painstaking hours spent on her manicure by scoring pointed, red-tipped fingernails down the length of his deceitful face.

'*Amour de mon coeur!*' The rough catch in his voice, the tenseness of his steel-sprung body, communicated urgent need. '*Amour de ma vie*, I had not meant to speak tonight, I felt it was too soon, that your delicious innocence has made you unprepared. But, as always,' a shudder of desire racked his strong frame, 'you have managed to confound me.' Violently he pulled her closer, so close that their shadows merged in urgent consummation. 'I want you, darling, *belle châtaigne*, please say that you will marry me.'

A cold clinical part of her brain clicked into action. With claws carefully sheathed, she ran her fingers down the length of his cheek until they rested tenderly upon a faint scar, newly healed, where her signet ring had branded her initials upon his lip.

'Brut, darling Brut ...' she sighed, projecting masterly conviction. 'I thought you would never ask me ... !'

CHAPTER TEN

'How are things in the vineyard, Louis?'

Louis' eyes lifted from his plate. It was breakfast time, but already he and Peter had put in a couple of hours work on the terraces. 'The fourth and fifth leaves are emerging from the shoots, Maman,' he told her with obvious satisfaction.

'Good.' With a heavy thump Hortense set down the coffee pot she had been wielding. 'Then it is time for the battle against pests and diseases to commence. Let us pray that the summer does not turn out to be particularly humid so that the minimum of seven sprayings need not be exceeded.'

'Exceeded!' Peter looked appalled. 'The thought of having to lug a ten-gallon drum of solution around the vineyard seven times in three months is bad enough! If you had allowed us to take Brut up on his offer,' he challenged Chantal, 'we would have been saved hours of heavy work. Even now it is not too late,' he urged, willing her to look at him, 'especially now that circumstances between you and him have so dramatically changed.'

She sensed that all three were waiting for her reply, each puzzled by her confusing reticence on the subject of the engagement that had been announced with startling suddenness by Brut two weeks ago on the night of the *bal masqué*. Since then he had paid her frequent and ardent attention, turning up each morning at the vineyard, spending as many hours as he could spare at the side of the girl he supposedly adored. What puzzled them most was the fact that while in his company she epitomised their ideal of a happy, radiant fiancée, yet immediately he left she assumed an attitude of detachment that could not be explained away as being the understandable reaction of a girl pining in the absence of her lover.

When Peter had attempted to tease her out of one of these moods his jocular remarks had been met with frozen solemnity. Hortense's one solicitous attempt to encourage confidences had evoked what could almost have been termed a snub. Even Louis' reproachful looks had prodded from her an uncharacteristic burst of irritation.

Shamefaced, knowing how unreasonable her actions must seem, she toyed with the food on her plate, wishing she could indulge in the luxury of unburdening her mind. But to whom? Hortense's initial reaction to the news of her engagement had been one of awed astonishment. 'Monsieur le Marquis ... ! *You* are to marry Monsieur le Marquis?' The implication that she should consider herself the most fortunate girl in the Province had been unmistakable. Then delight had taken over. 'Oh, mademoiselle!' she had clasped her hands together as if in joyful prayer. 'How clever of you to have captured so great a prize—and with such small a *dot*! How I wish your *grand'mère* were alive to bless the union.'

Peter, too, had displayed an astonishment that was less than flattering when, in the midst of a cheering throng whose excitement had been escalated by Brut's announcement, he had bent to kiss her cheek. 'Congratulations, dark horse,' he had murmured, then with the selfishness of youth that considers no one's affairs should take precedence over his own, he had turned her heart to stone with the hissed undertone, 'How do you feel about a double wedding?'

Not to one of them, not even Louis whose attachment was so strong his happiness had become dependent upon her moods, could Chantal confide how her flesh shrank from the caresses of a man who was demonstrating his possessiveness more and more plainly as each day went by, whose laughing face hid cunning deceit, whose murmured lies tortured her ears, whose enthusiasm as he outlined his plans for their future sounded so genuine she found herself having to fight a powerful current of persuasion by reminding herself time and time again of the cruel, shameless duplicity he was practising.

'Well,' Peter's sulky tone impinged upon her mind, 'as you don't seem disposed to help out in that respect, you'd better come with us to the vineyard—you can mix the compound while Louis and I do the spraying.'

Without comment, she followed them outside and began trekking in their wake, deliberately closing her ears to Peter's loud, pointed references to water storage tanks scattered around a neighbouring vineyard, and to the numerous small motorised tankers shuttling between the tanks and the vineyards to keep workers supplied with water.

By the time she had finished mixing her sixth batch of solution Chantal was feeling grateful for the sleeveless tee-shirt she had chosen to wear that

allowed the small amount of breeze available to cool
her skin as she toiled non-stop beneath the heat of
an early summer sun. She suspected spite in the
voraciousness of Peter's demands for more and more
solution to fill up the container he had strapped to
his back, and ignored his resentful mutterings as
time after time he was forced to retrace his steps,
scrambling along uneven paths, toiling up steep
slopes, in order to carry out the back-breaking task
of spraying the precious vines.

She was bending over a tank, stirring furiously
with a stick, when she felt the imprint of a kiss,
startling as a snakebite, stabbing the cool nape of
her neck. She whirled on her heel, caught too
quickly unawares to mask her resentment, or to bite
back the furious words that leapt to her tongue.

'Don't do that!' All the heat and frustration of
the day exploded into her words. 'I'm not a mere
thing to be mauled and played with at your whim,
I'm a *person*, and I'll thank you to treat me as
such!'

Brut stepped back with a soundless whistle and
stood rocking on his heels, examining her flushed,
rebellious face with narrowed eyes. 'Hardly the response one expects from a loving fiancée,' he rebuked mildly. Then with a sudden, heart-rocking
grin he confused her utterly. 'Are you aware of the
small army of freckles marching across your brow
and down the bridge of your pert little nose?' He
reached out as if impelled to trace their progress,
then, remembering her earlier reaction, changed his
mind and thrust his hand deep into the pocket of his
slacks.

Instinctively, her hand lifted to shield her face. 'Yes, I am aware of the hateful things,' she muttered brusquely, 'each summer I hope they won't appear, but invariably they erupt at the first hint of sunshine.'

'I'm glad they do,' he returned gently. 'On you, they look adorable.'

The quivering she dreaded erupted inside her, a deep yearning to respond that was the worst of the many agonies imposed by their farcical engagement. 'I read somewhere that you Frenchmen have an unlimited capacity for gallantry and that you indulge it on every occasion,' she snapped, too hot, bothered and untidy to continue with pretence. 'Why bother to waste your compliments on a drudge?'

His jaw tightened, yet his tone remained mild. 'Can't you recognise good old-fashioned courtship, *chérie*?'

To her dismay, tears flooded into her eyes. Unnerved by the gentle censure, she swung away to hide the tell-tale sign of weakness, expecting hard fingers to fasten upon her shoulders.

But he surprised her by remaining where he was, content to bridge the gap between them with a quietly-spoken yet compelling request.

'You have worked long enough for one day, Chantal. Leave what you are doing and get changed—I am taking you for a drive.'

It was typical of the man that he should choose such forceful words, to command rather than to invite, to say 'I am taking you' and not 'Would you like to come?' yet even so she experienced an unfamiliar sensation of being cosseted—for the first time in her life she was being led instead of leant upon.

'I can't.' Immediately she voiced the refusal she realised how much she wanted to go. 'Peter and Louis are relying upon my help.'

'I rather expected they might be,' his tone was dry, 'which is why I've brought along two of my estate workers to give them a hand. Even you, my spirited, red-haired Saxon, cannot claim to achieve a better output than two men. I will listen to no more of your arguments, I *insist*,' he placed silken stress, 'that you put down that stick to which you have become so attached and come with me!'

Smothering a shameful surge of relief, Chantal gave in to his dominance. Half an hour later, freshly bathed and dressed in a dress of springtime yellow, bright as crocus, spiked with leaves of green, she relaxed with an unconscious sigh of pleasure into the passenger seat of his luxurious car. She sensed his glint of satisfaction as he activated the controls that set the monster purring down the mountain road, but kept her eyes averted in the hope that he would not sense the lethargy that would make her easy prey to his will.

'Firstly, we will call in at the Château,' he surprised her by saying. 'I am having the main suite of rooms redecorated and would like you to choose the colour scheme for our bedroom.' Unaware of the shock to her senses, he continued smoothly, 'After that, I will take you on a tour of the grounds—they are looking beautiful at the moment, fresh, green, and bursting with new-born life. Would you like that?'

'May we . . .' she gulped. 'May we take a walk first of all?' The coward in her shied from sharing with him the intimacy of a bedroom, even though the excuse he had given for the visit was pure fabrication. 'It's such a glorious day it would be shameful to waste even a minute of it.'

'Even though sunshine is bound to increase your *taches de rousseur*?' he teased.

'Freckles may be the bane of my life, but I've learned to live with them,' she countered stiffly.

'I look forward to the day when I, too, may be permitted to enjoy such intimacy,' he admitted softly, directing her a smile that warned of a patience that was almost exhausted, the smile of a male temporarily tamed yet anxious to toss off his bridle of restraint. Her head jerked erect, sensing the presence of a predator. She could sense, smell, almost feel the current of vibrancy emanating from the man sitting relaxed in his seat with the smile of a victor playing around his mouth. In her highly sensitive state she would have scrambled out of her comfortable trap had they not been travelling so fast. As it was, she had no choice but to remain seated, striving to retain a look of cool composure in the hope that he would not guess that inwardly she was cowering.

He drove along the avenue of plane trees, round to the back of the Château, then parked the car outside an empty stable. Much against her will, he insisted upon taking her hand to guide her in the direction of a park that began as a garden and merged into woodland without any visible line of separation. Naturalness combined with grandeur was the dominating impression she gained as they strolled past a rush-fringed lake, hidden garden temples and across smooth lawns that splintered into woodland with such suddenness that before she was aware how it had happened she found that they had become isolated within a dense mass of trees, silent except for the occasional rustling of small animals in the undergrowth and the song of feathered tenors calling their mates. Sunshine penetrated the foliage, strewing dappled coins of gold along their path. Springy moss cushioned their footsteps as, still hand in hand, they penetrated farther into the wood, beckoned onward by the silvery tinkling of a hidden stream, sharing without words a sense of peace and tranquillity seldom encountered outside the womb.

Lulled into a false state of complacency, Chantal did not become aware of her folly until, with a flourish of triumph, Brut urged her forward into a clearing carpeted white with heavily scented flowers, lily of the valley, their fragile stems drooping beneath the weight of tiny bell-shaped flowers that were the symbol of purity.

'*La combe de Junon!*' he introduced her, pulling her into the path of glittering sunshine. 'Are you familiar with the legends of mythology?' When hesitantly she shook her head, he proceeded to enlighten her. 'Juno, goddess of light, was said to occupy an important part in the ceremonies of marriage and its consequent effects. Under many different titles, she was professed to watch over the arrangement of marriages; to conduct the bride to the house of her husband to ensure that she crossed the threshold; unknotted the bride's girdle, then later supplied protection to the pregnant wife. The lily,' he stooped to pick a flower and handed it to her, 'was long ago dedicated to the goddess Juno, which partly explains how this dell came by its name.' His teeth flashed white in a grin. 'There is a second, local legend attached to this dell. As Juno was known to be the goddess of light she was also, by derivation, goddess of childbirth, for the newborn baby is brought into the light. Childless couples travel for many miles just to make love within this magic circle and, if gossip can be believed, not one of them has yet found the journey unrewarding. Recently, an even more startling discovery has been mentioned—I speak from hearsay, you understand, never having tested out the theory I cannot vouch for its authenticity—according to the young bachelors of the area, the magic works just as well for couples lacking marital status.'

Chantal sought relief from unbearable tension in brittle flippancy. 'And is that the reason why you have brought me here—to test out a theory, one born of men without morals?'

Suddenly he jerked her into his arms. 'A Frenchman is first and foremost a *man*,' he retorted angrily, 'despicable, perhaps; weak, maybe, but always thoroughly *human*! But I am beginning to wonder if you are human, Chantal.' He shook her vigorously. 'Life for me these past weeks has been a long, tormenting hell, the hell of hope when you have melted against my heart, then the hell of despair when, even as my arms are holding you tightly, I sense your mental retreat—like candle smoke you drift through my fingers—and when in desperation I try to force you to respond I feel I am making love to a woman without substance, that my kisses are being blocked by a barrier of ice. Something is missing between us, Chantal! Why do you hold back, the chemistry will work for us, if you will allow it?'

Chemistry! Of course, to the Marquis, making love would be a clinical exercise. Physically, he could be aroused, so much so that at times the extent of his passions had kindled within her a response that was frightening, but always she had managed to retain sufficient sanity to remind herself that passion used as barter was worthless. He wanted her land and was prepared to cheat in order to get it—Trésor d'Hélène in exchange for meaningless words and worthless kisses!

Accusations trembled on her lips, the impulse to scathe, to storm, to scoff, was almost irresistible, but for Peter's sake it had to be subdued. Employing a deceit that was shamefully familiar, she melted against him and with her bright head resting against his heart, she murmured:

'I'm sorry, Brut, if I've been unfair to you. I have no right to allow personal worries to intrude on our relationship.'

'Personal worries ...?' He tightened his grip, completely hoodwinked. 'Everything we have, we must share, my love; your worries are mine. Tell me what it is that is troubling you.'

She dropped to her knees in a riot of flowers and when he sat down beside her she snuggled close, sighed, then in a soft, pleading whisper, admitted, 'It's Peter—he seems to have become infatuated with Nicole, and she's encouraging him. He ... he's even gone so far as to mention marriage.' She twisted round in his arms, her green eyes troubled. 'He's too young, Brut, and it will be many, many years before he's able to support a wife!'

He threw back his head and laughed. 'Are you telling me that I have been made to suffer the torment of the damned simply because of a young man's first love affair? Oh, *ma petite!*' he rocked her tenderly, 'when will you stop playing the protective mother so that your chick might develop wings? Dismiss him from your mind,' he urged softly. 'In time, Peter will develop in acordance with what is expected of him, but meanwhile he needs to experiment if he is ever to become emotionally mature. I remember my own first love affair,' he chuckled beneath his breath. 'She was a gypsy girl, one of a family which comes here every year to help gather in the harvest. She was voluptuous, vivacious, and very available. For a whole month I barely left her side, she taught me all that a young man needs to know,' he mused, 'and when the time came for her to leave I was convinced that my heart was broken. She still comes regularly to do the picking,' he digressed in order to kiss a freckle on the end of her nose, 'and now possesses blackened teeth, a thickened waistline, and a brood of dirty, ill-mannered children, yet still I feel a fondness for her—the sort of fondness a man always cherishes for the woman who initiated him into manhood.'

Though she had no illusions about Nicole's ability to survive, Chantal could not resist a prod. 'But what about your cousin's feelings, aren't you concerned on her behalf?'

'Nicole?' For a second she almost believed that he was as indifferent as he sounded. 'You need have no fears that her emotions will become involved, *chérie*. When that young woman marries she will be guided by her head, never by her heart.'

Chantal's own heart responded with a twist of pain to the cynical observation, stated with such certainty because he and his cousin were both of the same mind. Impelled by an impulse to be assured, to hear her suspicions confirmed by his own words, she took advantage of his mellow mood by pressing, 'Hortense tells me that you French don't always consider love to be a necessary part of marriage. Is she right? Would you marry if you were not in love?'

Tensely, she waited, burying her head into his chest so that it rose and fell in rhythm with his heart. She felt the imprint of his lips against her hair, and was surprised by the huskiness of his tone when, after a considerable silence, he admitted, 'There are times when I think I would have preferred to have been spared the emotional upheaval described as being in love. Loving takes away one's self-sufficiency because it involves a longing always to be with another person, a need to consider their wellbeing before one's own, a desire to be intimately and exclusively absorbed.' He tilted her chin until he was able to gaze deeply into her wondering eyes. Silently, he held her glance and she began to quiver, her emotions unbearably stretched by his masterful technique of seduction. He looked so solemn, his blue eyes so darkened with feeling, she almost fell into the trap of crediting his hoarsely whispered words with sincerity. 'When I am with you, *mon ange*, I feel deeply grateful for being allowed to share in the most dramatic and mysterious experience known to man!'

Her skirt had ridden, unnoticed, above her knees. Denied obstruction, he slid the palm of his hand along the length of her cool thigh, jerking her into fresh awareness of the danger she had sensed earlier. But the warning came too late to apply a brake on the emotions of a man who found her innocence irresistible, whose impulsive demands were crying out to be met—*now*!

Crushing her deep into the riot of fragrant blossoms, Brut cradled her within the crook of his arm, seemingly intent upon kissing each freckle in turn, his lips progressing along the soft curve of her cheek, across her brow, down the bridge of her pert nose, murmuring soft assurances to soothe the fear that had sprung into her eyes. Gently, his light caressing touch roved the curves of her body, igniting beacons of fire at the tip of every rioting nerve, draining her of strength, of the will to resist.

'Relax, my startled fawn,' he breathed against the tender hollow of her throat, 'there is no need to fear the pleasures of love. *Je me consume pour toi!* Darling Chantal, prove to me that you love me!'

The demand jerked her to her senses—man's oldest ploy, used since the days of Adam—if you love me, give me your body!

She stiffened in his arms so that despite the heat of passion, despite the euphoria created by the strong fragrance rising from their bed of crushed and broken flowers he became aware of her cold withdrawal.

'What's wrong, *mon ange*?'

The urgent question enraged her, coming as it did from a man who, not content to trick her out of her inheritance, wanted her body as well. It called for great effort of will to employ the use of strategy. Directing him a deliberately sorrowful look, she reproached quietly:

'It is because I love you so much that I cannot allow myself to make such a mistake,' she lied. 'You value only what is unique, Brut. In your house full of treasures there is not one piece of cracked porcelain, not one precious wood carving that carries a blemish, not a single item that is not beautiful, flawless and unmarked. On the day that I enter the Château as your bride,' she whispered, 'I want to feel certain that I am cherished above all the treasures that you possess ...'

CHAPTER ELEVEN

'Where is Monsieur le Marquis taking you today?' Hortense enquired.

'To visit the cellars.' Chantal's reply was absent, her mind busy with the problem of what to wear.

'*Très bon!* You will enjoy that.' When Chantal made no reply Hortense's tongue clicked with annoyance. 'Sometimes I suspect you do not appreciate the extent of your good fortune, mademoiselle, do not fully realise how rarely one encounters a man who is so thoughtful and kind. In this region, it is common for most men to place a hard-working wife first in their priorities, yet the Marquis is always insisting that you take plenty of rest and even sent two of his own men to work permanently with Peter and Louis once he discovered that, although the announcement of your engagement had the required effect upon the locals, the news came too late to prevent all the best workers from promising their services to other vineyards. Next year they will be queuing at our door,' she promised grimly, 'then it will be our turn to be choosey!' Her face brightened. 'What a handsome bridegroom the Marquis will make! Have you noticed, mademoiselle, how many tall, fair-haired, blue-eyed men there are in Champagne? They are descendants of the men of the north—the original inhabitants of Champagne.'

'Really ...?' Chantal was still preoccupied. What

to wear on outings with Brut—that had become more and more frequent since the day of their traumatic clash in the woods behind the Château—was now not merely a problem but more of a dilemma. The contents of her wardrobe consisted of a few outfits so well worn they were on the verge of looking shabby. Brut was always so immaculately and tastefully dressed she was beginning to feel ashamed of being seen in his company. Not that he ever seemed to notice any deficiencies in her dress, quite the reverse, in fact, for whenever they were together his absorbed, attentive eyes never strayed from her face. She found the experience unnerving. He had accepted her ultimatum, but as he was perfectly well aware that her promise would never reach fruition, she suspected that he was holding himself constantly on the alert for any sign of weakening on her part. Quite by accident, she had hit upon the one challenge he could not ignore—since it had been made plain to him that she was unavailable he began to desire her desperately!

The outfit she finally decided upon was a sundress made of cool, cream cotton with knife-pleated skirt, a strapless bodice and a small bolero to shrug over her bare shoulders if the weather should become cool. A narrow, tan-coloured belt—almost the shade of her hair—made her waist look tiny and drew Brut's attention the moment she stepped inside the room into which Hortense had shown him.

'You look delicious—good enough to eat,' he greeted with a smile, showing typical male ignorance of outdated fashion, 'like a creamy sundae with a nut on top.' He lowered his head. 'May I be permitted a bite of the cherry?' he asked, his eyes fastened upon ripe red lips.

Dutifully, Chantal tilted her mouth upwards and waited with eyes closed to experience the sweet, surging thrill his kisses never failed to arouse.

'Forget it, Chantal.' Her eyes flew open at the distant sound of his voice and widened even further when she saw that he was standing at the far side of the room, clenched fists dug deeply into his pockets. 'Duty tastes as sour as the grape of the wild vine,' he told her bleakly. 'I'll wait a little longer and perhaps reap the sweetness of a cultivated harvest.'

She maintained a hurt, puzzled silence as they drove in summer sunshine through landscape whitened as if by a fall of snow, every hill and field shrouded in a veil of powdered chalk that shifted with each gust of wind and rose in furious puffs around the feet of men and grazing animals—the chalk upon which the whole of the district was built.

Brut made no attempt to break the silence until the butter-coloured edifice of the Château loomed in front of them. The road was deserted when he drew the car to the side of the road and switched off the engine.

'I have a present for you,' he surprised her by saying, reaching into his pocket to withdraw a small leather-bound box. When he released a spring the lid flew open, revealing a ring so huge, so deeply green, it could only be made of paste. Reaching for her hand, he slid her signet ring from her third finger and replaced it with the heavy, cumbersome stone, then, keeping her hand cupped within his palm, he elevated one sharply defined eyebrow, awaiting her comments.

Wondering what exactly he was expecting of her, she struggled for words, discarding delighted adjectives as being too hypocritical, feeling annoyed that he could consider her naïve enough to be deceived by such vulgar imitation.

'Well, have you nothing to say?' He seemed surprised by her prolonged silence.

'Oh ... er ... it's very nice,' she stammered, 'very nice indeed.' She began twisting her wrist to display the ring at different angles, wondering what more she could say about the beastly object.

He sat back in his seat looking disappointed, as if he had expected a far more favourable reaction. But how could he? she asked herself. How dared he expect that she would be fooled by a so very obvious sham?

'May I keep this?' Her signet ring looked fragile hooked around the first joint of his little finger.

A denial sprang to her lips. The ring had been a present from her father and as such was precious to her, yet for some inexplicable reason she could not refuse his request even though, after she had gone, it would most likely be tossed into a drawer and forgotten as easily as *she* would be forgotten.

'If you wish,' she gulped. 'It's of very little value.'

'I will carry it always in the pocket nearest my heart,' he assured her with deceptive gravity. When he lifted the ring to his lips her heart gave a sudden lurch. 'To me, it will always remain priceless, treasured because it is a part of you.'

As if anxious not to tire her, he started up the car, to continue their journey towards the Château. 'My aunt, Nicole's mother, is anxious to meet you,' he told her, swinging the car into the avenue of plane trees, 'so I invited her to join us here this morning. I expect she will be waiting inside.'

Every sensitive nerve cringed from the thought of having to be polite to the woman Chantal knew was her enemy. As Brut ushered her into the Château and across the hall she clenched her fists, steeling herself for the encounter.

They discovered Madame Mortemart sitting at a table set out on a terrace thickly fringed with ferns and cooled by the shade of tall trees bordering a baize-smooth lawn dotted with colourful flower beds. She looked exactly as Chantal had imagined, intimidatingly assured in a suit easily recognisable as an elegant creation of one of the leading fashion houses. Predictably, it was black—the colour most favoured by mature Frenchwomen—its severity only slightly relieved by a silken grey and white blouse, its neckline filled by a three-strand necklace of pearls. On one lapel a diamond brooch glittered —hard and bright as the stare directed by the silver-haired woman who rose to her feet with the lissom ease of a girl.

But a deeply-scored brow and lines of dissatisfaction pulling down the edges of her mouth betrayed bitter discontent.

'So you are Mademoiselle Barry whom I have heard so much about?' Her expression became transformed the moment Brut effected an introduction. 'May I please be allowed to call you Chantal?

The likeness between yourself and your late *grand'-mère* is so pronounced that already I feel I have known you for a very long time.'

'I would be honoured, Madame.' Chantal quaked, inwardly repelled by a hypocrisy that welcomed with a smile that was not reflected in eyes hard with rancour. 'You knew my grandmother well?' She dropped into the seat Brut had drawn forward, thankful for its support against her trembling knees.

The other woman's eyebrows rose. 'Has no one mentioned that for many years I acted as your grandmother's companion? I was also her private secretary, her *confidante*, sharing in everything—her hopes, her fears,' delicately, she hesitated, 'and in the great sadness caused by the rift between your mother and herself. No one knows better than I the great pain she suffered when time after time the letters she wrote, or rather that I wrote to her dictation, remained unanswered. It was *très tragique*, don't you think, that your mother was never able to forgive?'

Stiffly ill at ease, Chantal fought to find excuses for her parents' behaviour, but she could think of none. If, as Madame Mortemart had so positively stated, the old Comtesse had subdued her pride and written not once but many times in an attempt to bridge the separation, then her parents' refusal to respond was inexcusable. She lapsed into embarrassed silence, willing Brut, who had moved out of earshot, to come to her rescue.

It seemed as if her mute signal had reached him when he strode towards them carrying a dark, gold-foiled bottle.

'Champagne!' Chantal could not help sounding rather shocked. 'Isn't it rather early in the day?'

'The first mid-morning glass tastes the best of any,' Brut assured her with a grin. 'According to Madame de Pompadour it is the only wine that leaves a woman beautiful after drinking it, lending a sparkle to the eye, but leaving the skin unflushed. Not that I expect any improvement in you, *chérie,* your freckled beauty could never, in my opinion, be surpassed.'

Conscious of his aunt's hard stare, Chantal concentrated her attention upon Brut as expertly he removed the gold foil from around the cork, twisted off a wire muzzle, then holding the base of the bottle in one hand and the cork in the other, with his thumb over the top, he gently twisted both base and cork in opposite directions. She tensed for the expected loud pop but was surprised when the cork and the bottle parted company with little more than a sigh.

Correctly interpreting her expression, Brut smiled. 'It is also unnecessary to swathe the bottle in a white napkin. Why should we go to the bother of supplying an extravagant package if it is not meant to be shown?' With a steady wrist he poured a stream of pale gold liquid into fluted glasses, then lifted one of them aloft so that she could see the host of tiny bubbles streaming upwards.

He took time to pass a glass of wine to his aunt, together with a plate of sweet biscuits, but turned immediately back to Chantal to clink the rim of his glass against hers, holding her eyes with a look so

intense it was easy to forget they were not completely alone.

'Dare you sip the devil's wine, *mon ange*?' he
queried softly, tiny flames leaping in the depths
of his eyes.

Controlling a swift blush of awareness, she lifted
the tall misted glass to her lips and as she sipped felt
bubbles breaking beneath her nose and sniffed a
fragrant bouquet that went straight to her head.
'The devil seeks slaves and claims obedience,' she
quipped, hating her own inane, nervous giggle. 'I'm
not sure that I'm prepared to pay so dear a price.
However, I expect some exchange will have to be
made for indulging in the wicked extravagance of
drinking champagne while early morning sun
shines.'

'We French drink champagne when we feel like
it, *chérie*,' his aunt's voice broke into their absorption. 'You will learn,' she paused to smile thinly, 'if
you are with us long enough, that *le vin diable* is not
reserved purely for festive occasions.'

Unnerved by the animosity the older woman was
projecting, Chantal gulped down wine that had
turned sour in her mouth and made to return her
glass to the table. But her hand holding the glass
was shaking so much she raised the other hand to
steady it, bringing into full view the huge stone
glowing emerald green in the sunlight.

Madame Mortemart's scandalised gasp was clearly
audible. 'Brut!' she exclaimed, seemingly mesmer-
ised by the ring. 'Why is she wearing the La Roque
emerald?'

'Why should she not?' Lazily, Brut smiled into

Chantal's startled eyes. 'The emerald is an heirloom that for centuries has been presented by the men of my family to their prospective brides. Naturally, I have followed tradition by presenting the La Roque emerald to the girl who has promised to be my wife.'

With visible effort of will, his aunt regained her composure, nevertheless, damped-down anger smouldered in her eyes when, with thin lips barely moving, she charged Chantal, 'You realise, I hope, that the emerald you are wearing is one of the few of its size in the world that is completely flawless and that it is therefore priceless?' Luckily for Chantal, whose vocal cords, in common with the rest of her, were paralysed with shock, she did not wait for an answer but stabbed out a second hard statement. 'It is very important that you realise also that in addition to its monetary value the emerald is of great sentimental value and must always remain with the family. What I am telling you is this. When,' quickly, she amended, '*should* your betrothal ever be terminated there is no question of your ever being allowed to retain possession of the ring.'

After she had stridden rigid-backed from the room Chantal withdrew the huge emerald from her finger and laid it carefully upon the table.

'I thought it was made of paste,' she quavered, 'otherwise I would never have dared to wear it. Why didn't you explain its history?'

'I eventually would have done so, but that aspect did not seem important at the time,' Brut clipped, looking angrier than she had ever seen him. 'Please excuse my aunt's interference. Over the years I have allowed her too great a say in my affairs, with the result that she now seems to consider herself blessed with unlimited licence. I shall insist that you receive an apology.'

Noting his rock-hard jaw, the steel hardness of his eyes, she felt a sneaking sympathy for his aunt. 'She was quite rightly trying to protect your interest,' she pointed out gently, 'and I'm glad she did. Now that I know the truth I can't possibly take responsibility for its safe keeping.'

'The truth?' His hand flashed out to grip her chin, forcing her to endure a look of probing anger. 'When have I ever lied to you, Chantal?' His effrontery made her gasp. Their whole relationship was built upon lies, he and Nicole had evolved a coldly calculated plan to ruin her own and Peter's future, yet he dared to ask such a question!

Nevertheless, because the finale was not yet in sight the farce had to be played out. 'The fault may have been mine,' she stammered. 'I misunderstood, jumped to the conclusion that because of its size the jewel had to be sham.'

'You actually thought that I would mark our betrothal with a ring that was not genuine?' His low monotone had more impact than a furious tirade. When dropped lashes conveyed her shame he condemned over the top of her bent head, 'I suspect there are other misconceptions harbouring behind your cool shell. Would this not be a good time to begin sorting them out? You have been proved wrong once, Chantal, and could be again.' Swiftly he swooped upon the ring and thrust it back upon her finger. 'Wear it!' he ordered. 'Let

its presence act as a reminder that you have promised to be my bride.'

During the short time it took to drive from the
Château to the site of the wine cellars she had time
to think and was amazed at the ease with which
he had managed to fill her mind with doubts and
uncertainty. The idea of having felt shame on his
behalf was, with hindsight, so ludicrous she almost
laughed aloud. How he must be ejoying manipulat-
ing her emotions, she thought bitterly, how amused
he must be by her naïveté, how satisfied with his
success! But success breeds complacency, she consoled herself. Keeping the beast complacent would
help to hasten his downfall.

Though everything about the Champagne country interested her, what lay beneath was astonishing.
'The ageing of bottled wine has to take place very
slowly,' Brut explained, 'and in a very cool place
devoid of draughts, because any abrupt change of
temperature can cause the bottles to explode.'

In the cellars running like rabbit warrens beneath
the towns and villages of the district conditions were
ideal. Chantal shivered as he led her through vast
galleries hewn out of chalk centuries earlier by
slaves carrying out the orders of conquering Ro-
mans. Alert, as always, to her needs, Brut shrugged
off his jacket and slipped it around her shoulders,
then without removing his arm he guided her
through long underground tunnels holding thous-
ands of neatly racked bottles.

His voice echoed through pyramid-shaped caverns
as he urged her to keep tight hold of wrought iron
rails edging each flight of steep dimly-lighted steps,

and instructed her on the processes undergone by the wine before it was ready for marketing. They walked from cellar to cellar, each one more awe-inspiring than the last, great vaults of chalk with light projecting through scrolled ironwork so that decorative panels filtering against dark surfaces seemed to hang like paintings on the walls of a dim, silent cathedral.

'So many bottles!' she gasped, more than a little bemused by the realisation that the work carried out in the vineyards was a mere preliminary to many hours of labour by many workers concerned not merely with the processing but also with a vast range of work that was less glamorous yet equally vital—the maintenance of ventilating shafts that permitted air to circulate; of water pipes that enabled the cellars to be kept clean; of drainage systems that carried off used water and the spillage from broken bottles, the lifts that needed to be kept in working order, the staircases, ramps and tunnels that needed to be maintained in tip-top condition to ensure that the movement of bottles from cellar to cellar was accomplished easily and smoothly.

But the best and most delightful surprise Brut kept to the last. 'Close your eyes,' he instructed, halting outside a heavy wooden door that was barely discernible through the gloom of a chalk tunnel. Unmoved by her questioning look, he refused further explanation and waited with a half smile playing around his lips until she did as he had asked.

With a mystified shrug she obeyed, and remained with lashes downcast wondering what further surprise was in store. She heard the sound of a key turning in a lock, the creak of hinges as the door swung open, then felt his hand upon her elbow urging her forward.

'You may open them now.' His tone of whimsical indulgence increased her curiosity. Her lids flew upwards, then widened as she stepped inside a chalk grotto flooded with delicate blue light. It was empty except for a pedestal holding a jewel-encrusted statue of the Virgin and Child expertly positioned so that hidden spotlights played upon the Madonna's face, highlighting an expression of devoted motherhood that seemed uncannily human. The folds of her dress seemed to move in the draught from the doorway, as did the hand of the infant stretching out to clutch His mother's shawl.

'How ...? Why ...?' she gasped, awe-filled eyes fixed upon the exquisite tableau.

'The statue is very old,' he told her, 'so we are not certain of its precise origin. It came into the possession of the House as a wedding present given many years ago to the bride of one of the partners. For years it was housed in the Château, then some forty years ago some inspired person designed this unique and special setting hundreds of feet below ground.' His arm slid around her shoulders as softly he murmured, 'Each time I look at it I am reminded of the saying: "There is no slave out of heaven like a loving woman, and of all loving women there is no such slave as a mother."'

Chantal's mouth felt suddenly dry. His words held a message that turned her bones to water, yet she resented the intrusion of further deceit into an interlude of deep reverence.

Brut frowned when a shudder racked her slim body. Swiftly he tightened his arm, hugging her closer to his side. 'I ought to have remembered to warn you about the coolness of the cellars. We will return to the surface; you have shivered long enough.'

Feeling in no mood to argue, she allowed him to lead her back to the surface where in the bright light of day the tenseness of her expression was mistaken for regret.

'We will come back another day when you are better prepared,' he assured her, sounding slightly teasing. 'But if you would like to continue your exploration perhaps my laboratory would be of interest?'

The invitation could not have been broached more casually, yet she sensed that he was pleased by the eagerness she forced into her acceptance. 'May I be permitted to visit the holy of holies? According to Hortense, few outsiders are allowed admittance to the sanctuary of a *chef de cave*!'

'I'm sorry to have to disappoint you,' he grinned wryly, 'but the reason visitors are discouraged is because there is so little to be seen. I admit that when I am working it is vital that the air around me does not become polluted by cigarette smoke, perfume, and suchlike, but otherwise my surroundings are completely unremarkable.'

Reminded that she had once again acted upon her grandmother's advice and applied a liberal amount of perfume, Chantal made a small moue of disappointment. 'In that case ...' she began.

'I know,' he interrupted. 'The reminder of woods

in springtime has teased my nostrils all morning, but as this is not one of my working days the only havoc caused will be to my senses.'

The laboratory was situated nearby, a bare brick building set close to the entrance to the caves. Her first impression when she stepped inside was one of light, air, and clinical simplicity. Strictly functional furnishings—chairs, cupboards, a table scattered with an assortment of unidentifiable utensils—completed a scene totally lacking in comfort.

'What were you expecting to see?' he queried, amused by her downcast expression.

'Oh, fiery jets ... hissing steam ... glass cauldrons full of bubbling liquid,' she trailed vaguely, then faltered, suddenly conscious of how ridiculous the description must have sounded.

She chanced a shamefaced glance and found, just as she had expected, that his face had creased into laughter.

'At times I have been accused by jealous competitors of being something of a sorcerer,' he assured her, 'but I'm afraid the success of my blend is achieved by a mundane combination of a degree in bio-chemistry, good eyes, a sensitive nose, and a well trained palate. I wish I could live up to your illusion that I am some kind of wizard skilled in the mixing of magic potions, but unfortunately I can claim to be nothing other than a mere male.'

Her lips were quirking by the time he had finished mocking her naïveté, but as their laughing eyes held humour faded, leaving the room full of silent tension.

'Chantal .. !' he groaned, jerking her into his

arms. '*Je me consume pour toi!* You must admit that I have been good—how much longer must I wait until I receive my reward?'

'*Reward!*' The word acted like a bright green warning light. Rewards were sought in exchange for favours—obviously the ring she had received from him had been given not as a present but as a bribe! 'Ought I to feel flattered to be considered fair exchange for the family bauble?'

With his lips pressed against a pulse throbbing in her throat he went suddenly still. Slowly his head lifted to scour her pale, resentful face, then with wordless revulsion he pushed her aside and strode out of the room.

For a long time after he had gone she stood by a window battling with a threat of hot, shamed tears. 'He's a beast,' she assured herself fiercely, 'a selfish, unfeeling brute, a consummate actor capable of convincing without words that he has suffered deep and irrevocable hurt ...!'

CHAPTER TWELVE

THE grapes were beginning to ripen. For almost two months Chantal had existed with nerves on a knife edge, her personal problems aggravated by a tension that was being felt throughout the vineyards as anxiety mounted about the constant danger of late frosts damaging the vines. An abundance of fruit depended upon successful pollination; if a heavy frost should occur while the vines were flowering disaster was inevitable.

Tempers at Trésor d'Hélène had worn decidedly ragged, but as the days had grown progressively warmer, the atmosphere more humid, tension had eased, faces had begun to smile again. Now, the dried-up remains of flowers had been dispersed, small green pellets of fruit had ballooned almost to the size of maturity, and skins were gradually starting to change colour.

Concerned that Chantal's pinched features still showed signs of strain, Hortense had told her, 'You need worry no longer, mademoiselle, all that we now require for a successful harvest is as much warmth and sunshine as *le bon dieu* can provide.'

Chantal had felt like screaming aloud. No need to worry! Her life had developed into a disastrous mess, her emotions tortured each morning by a visit from an outwardly affable, outwardly solicitous fiancé whose cool kiss of greeting was a cross that

was becoming harder and harder to bear. Why he
bothered to keep up such pretence was a mystery.
Not once during the past weeks had he attempted
the least move towards intimacy, not once had he
pressed her to change her mind when she had de-
clined to accept invitations proffered with a casual
indifference she found insulting. Yet still he persis-
ted in trying to preserve an illusion that nothing
had changed between them, lulling any embryo suspicions Peter or Hortense might have harboured
by dropping into the conversation odd references
to alterations that were in progress at the Château
supposedly for the benefit of his new bride. His
clever insinuations had not gone unrewarded, for
in spite of lack of confirmation, Hortense and Peter
seemed to have concluded that the wedding was
to take place in autumn once the harvest had been
gathered.

Chantal had fretted and puzzled over his motives,
wondering how much longer she could endure having this blond, blue-eyed Adonis striding into her
life each morning—wondering when, if ever, the
devious Marquis would provide proof of his own
and his cousin's duplicity.

She was standing gazing out of the kitchen window, so could not avoid seeing Peter exchanging a
prolonged and affectionate farewell with Nicole. In
common with her cousin, she rode over to Trésor
d'Hélène most days with the sole object, Chantal
had no doubt, of ensuring that her victim remained
firmly pinned beneath a weight of adolescent adora-
tion. She squirmed when, as she watched, Nicole
reached out to stroke Peter's cheek, then stood on

tiptoe to tease his youthful ardour with a final kiss.

She felt barely able to restrain a torrent of angry condemnation when her brother strode into the kitchen.

'Can you spare a moment, Sis?' He hooked a lanky leg across a kitchen chair.

'I can,' she told him tartly, 'but can you? Do you think it's fair to leave so much of the work to Louis?'

'That's what I want to talk to you about.' To her amazement she saw that he was blushing to the roots of his hair, his youthful frame stiff with embarrassment. She braced to combat the outpouring of infatuated words that seemed inevitable, telling herself that she must not fall into the trap of showing animosity towards Nicole, but must employ gentle reason, appeal to his sense of responsibility as she tried to outline the pitfalls of an early marriage.

But his first words took the wind out of her sails. 'It's Nicole,' he blurted. 'I don't seem to be able to make her understand that a chap's work has to take precedence, especially at this time of the year. I know she tries to be helpful,' he jerked, running a harassed finger around the inside of his collar, 'but I waste more time than enough getting her out of difficulties, dancing attendance.' Glaring at Chantal as if she were the cause of his problem, he accused hotly, 'Why can't women understand how important a man's work is to him? My life, my whole future, is tied up in viticulture, yet when I try to explain how essential it is that jobs are finished on schedule she just laughs and teases and tries to coax me to leave the work to Louis and go off with her for the day. As the wife of a vineyard owner she'd be impossible!' he exploded. Colouring, if possible, a shade deeper, he fixed his eyes upon his shuffling feet. 'And there's something else,' he mumbled, acutely embarrassed. 'She keeps going on and on about marriage! When she first brought the subject up I thought it was rather a lark, so I played along,' his head jerked up to fix eyes full of anxious pleading on her face, 'but Nicole is taking it all so seriously, Sis! I don't want to get married!' Panic showed in his movements as he jerked to his feet. 'But how can I say so outright? She's so sweet, so tender, so loving, I couldn't possibly hurt her. You're an expert in these matters, please tell me what to do!'

Chantal wanted to dance and sing and cheer, if she had been wearing a bonnet she would have tossed it into the air. As it was she had to struggle to retain an expression of composure. Dropping her lashes to hide the bright, exhultant sparkle in her eyes, she began gently:

'I'm pleased you've felt able to tell me about it, Peter. I can understand how you must feel faced with a seemingly insoluble problem, but believe me,' she reached out to clasp his hand, 'you have no need to worry.'

'No need to worry!' With an incredulous look he snatched his hand away. 'How can you say that?'

'Because being a woman myself, I understand the working of a woman's mind,' she insisted firmly. Determined, at this delicate stage of the proceedings, not to upset him by disparaging Nicole, she continued, tongue in cheek, 'Nicole is a young and inexperienced girl. You, being more mature, were the first to realise that marriage between you two wouldn't work, but given time Nicole would also have arrived at the same conclusion. All girls of her age fall in love with the idea of getting married —at the moment she thinks she's in love with you, but actually she's just infatuated with the thought of wearing a wedding ring.'

'You think that's all there is to it?' he breathed, an expression of hope lightening his features.

'I'm sure of it,' she nodded. 'All you need do is be less available, less anxious to rush to her side— even arrange to be out a couple of times when you know she's due to call. After a few weeks of such treatment she'll become disillusioned and your appeal as a husband will gradually diminish.'

Looking infinitely relieved, Peter promised with respectful awe, 'I'll never underestimate you again, Sis. I can almost believe your plan will work!' He flung his arms wide, flexing his shoulder muscles as if relieved of an intolerable burden. 'Suddenly the future seems full of possibilities—thanks to you and Brut.'

'Brut ...?' She queried, her smile rather fixed. 'What part has he to play in your future?'

Made complacent by the knowledge that she could hardly object to his discussing their affairs with the man she was about to marry, Peter confided, 'Brut has suggested that in order to further my career I should attend a college of viticulture and oenology. He's also promised that if I do,' he paused to suck in an exultant breath, 'I can look forward to joining the Etablissement as his personal pupil *chef de cave*!'

Chantal's short span of happiness came to an abrupt end. Shaken by the depths of the Marquis's duplicity, she sank into a chair and managed to gasp, 'And what, might I ask, is to happen to the Trésor d'Hélène? You can't expect Louis and me to manage the vineyard on our own while you go off to college.'

'Of course not!' He looked astounded at the very thought. 'Brut will send in his own workers—you needn't worry about Hortense and Louis—he's promised that their position will remain unchanged. The price he's offered for the vineyard is more than ample to cover the cost of my education and to tide me over until I'm ready to join the staff of the Etablissement. Thank goodness, your future presents no problems—once you're Brut's wife your well-being will be assured.'

Chantal sat well into the early hours of the next morning huddled in an armchair in her bedroom, brooding over the clever tactics employed by the Marquis. With infinite cunning he had turned the tables on both herself and Nicole; like pieces on a chessboard, he had manoeuvred each of them into exactly the position needed to enable him to achieve victory.

Peter must have posed the least problem of all. By pandering to his enthusiasm for the work he loved, the Marquis had won him over with promises of an interesting and profitable career. Annoyingly, she could find no flaw in such a scheme, for its benefits ran exactly parallel to the ambitions she had nurtured on his behalf.

For Nicole, she felt little sympathy—was, indeed, glad that her plan to blackmail the Marquis into marriage had been neatly annihilated.

The only one of his pawns deserving of sympathy was herself. What was to happen to her once the farcical engagement had been broken off? She could not refuse to sell her share of the vineyard because to do so would be to jeopardise Peter's future, which was unthinkable. Where would she live? Their house in England had been let furnished and would not become available for at least two years and, once the Marquis took over control, the door of Trésor d'Hélène would no doubt be closed to her.

Refusing to wallow in self-pity, she jumped to her feet and began pacing the floor. She was beaten, frustrated, but even with her back to the wall she would fight until there was no breath left in her body. *The wary bachelor*, Nicole had called the Marquis, implying that he was a man who guarded his freedom jealously. No doubt, before asking her to marry him, he had carefully weighed up the odds and concluded that they were all in his favour. If they had not been, nothing would have induced him to risk his freedom. Well, he was the last man in the world she wanted to marry, *but he did not know that*, nor would he know it until she had made him squirm!

She came to an abrupt halt in the middle of the floor, her heart pumping madly. She would call his bluff! Make him sweat under the illusion that she intended to keep him to his promise, right up until the day of their proposed marriage! Then, at the very last moment, she would fling the deeds of the land in his face before storming out of his life, destitute of everything—except pride.

If Brut was surprised by the warmth of her greeting the following morning he did not show it. Following his usual custom, he bent his head to brush a kiss across her cheek but found himself instead kissing lips that had turned eagerly towards him. He took time to relish the unexpected offering, prolonging the kiss until Hortense began to chuckle and Chantal tore out of his arms, scarlet-faced.

Shaken to the core by the message he had secretly communicated, she avoided his glinting eyes and questioned nervously, 'Have you made any special plans for today?'

'No, I am yours to command,' he mocked, keeping narrowed eyes trained upon her face.

Determined to confound him, she forced brightness into her reply. 'I would like to see how work is progressing at the Château. There's so much to be done—do you realise,' boldly she challenged him, 'that we haven't yet set a firm date for our wedding day?'

This time he really was surprised. Emotion flared in his eyes—bright, startling, but unreadable. Confident that his reaction was one of dismay, her optimism soared to such heights that she was able to ask Hortense, 'Do you suppose we could take a second look at my grandmother's wedding dress? I should love to be able to wear it. With a little alteration here and there I feel certain it will fit. Oh, and another thing, Brut!' she was enjoying herself so much she had begun to sound quite imperious, 'Do you think your aunt would help me to get up a list of wedding guests?'

'I'm certain she would be delighted.' His reply was smooth but the look in his eyes remained keen. 'She and Nicole are holding one of their many committee meetings at the Château, if we hurry we might catch them before they leave.'

Chantal expected an inquisition about her change of attitude as they drove towards the Château, but he surprised her by generalising about the weather, the state of the crops, and the expected size of the harvest, touching lightly upon each topic, progressing with such smoothness from one to another that no break occurred in the conversation throughout the short journey.

She sensed that the ploy was deliberate, that he wanted no showdown to erupt—just yet. Consequently, her nerves felt as brittle as the laughter with which she responded to some quip as he helped her from the car.

The committee meeting was still in progress, they were told as they entered the hall. 'Please ask Madame Mortemart to speak with me before she leaves,' Brut requested the servant who had greeted them at the door, then he took Chantal's hand to lead her through the *salon* and outside on to the terrace where they had sat once before.

'Are you in the mood for further wickedness?' When her lashes flew up over guilty eyes, he qualified with a faintly mocking smile, 'Would you like a glass of champagne?'

'Oh . . . are you having one?'

'*Certainement.*' He moved towards an ice bucket and withdrew a gold-foiled bottle from a nest of cracked ice. 'I have no qualms about indulging myself, whatever the time of day or night, providing the experience is pleasant.'

As the cork sighed from its resting place she watched a spiral of vapour hovering momentarily before dispersing into the atmosphere. Carefully, he poured a measure of champagne into each of two glasses, then passed her one, instructing, 'Grip the stem of the glass tightly with the thumb, index, and middle fingers, then twirl it briskly, so that the wine is thoroughly disturbed from its slumbers.' When she did as he had requested he continued, 'Now, beginning with the eyes, test the appeal of the wine to your senses. Is the froth snow-white? Is the colour good?'

'Exactly what colour should it be?' she quavered, almost seduced by the mellow timber of his voice.

'Good champagnes come in a vast range of shades, from the paleness of straw to the bright bronze that tips your lashes,' he brooded down at her. 'But it should never be insipid, if the colour is not sharp and pleasing then the wine is imperfect.'

She tingled with awareness when he enclosed her hand in his, but he was merely urging her hand upwards so that the bubbles in her glass laughed down at her. 'See,' he nodded, 'how the bubbles form right down at the base of the stem, then shoot upwards to the surface? Now listen.' He guided her hand until the glass was resting against her ear, then fell silent.

'I can hear the bubbles crackling!' she cried, delighted by the discovery.

His smile reached to the depth of her soul. 'Champagne!' he toasted in a whisper, clicking the rim of his glass against hers, 'the only wine possessed of the ingredients essential to a perfect love affair—a touch of wickedness, a hint of fun!'

Their absorption was broken by a polite cough. 'Excuse me for interrupting,' his aunt walked on to the terrace, her gimlet eyes taking stock of the uncorked bottle, the half-filled glasses, and two heads close as one. 'I believe, Brut, that you wish to speak with me.'

'Not I—Chantal.' He stood up to peck the cheek his aunt proffered.

'Oh, yes . . . ?' She placed questioning emphasis on the two short words.

When Chantal floundered, utterly incapable of finding a suitable opening, he came to her rescue. 'We were wondering if you would like to help compile a list of names of all those who you think ought to be invited to attend our wedding.'

His aunt stepped backwards, obviously stricken. 'You cannot be serious?'

Looking decidedly vexed, he returned curtly, 'But of course I am—have you ever known me to joke about serious subjects? Chantal and I,' he pulled her close into his side, 'are to be married in the autumn. If for some reason you do not wish to assist us with the arrangements then kindly say so.'

Noting the look of shock in his aunt's eyes, Chantal guessed that it was the first time that he had ever spoken to her in such a harsh manner. For a moment her face worked as if she was about to burst into tears, but then she drew in a deep breath and relieved her anger by directing an outburst of venom towards Chantal.

'You cannot marry this girl—this *upstart*! Have you forgotten that she is the child of parents who broke the Comtesse's heart? That she is the child of the woman who humiliated your own father? Both she and her brother are here under false pretences,' she hissed, 'scroungers, both of them! But she,' she pointed a shaking finger at Chantal, 'is the worst of the two, a devious brat just like her mother!' Her eyes, full of hatred, speared Chantal. 'To bear two children, then fade from the scene leaving the bother of their upbringing to others, was typical of spoiled, mollycoddled Camille d'Estrées!'

Chantal flinched and was drawn tight against Brut's side. But the significance of his aunt's remark did not register until, in a deadly cold voice, Brut questioned:

'Would you mind telling me how you knew that Chantal's mother had died young? My father was not aware of it, I'm sure of that, and neither was the Comtesse, so how did you come by the information?'

For a fraction of a second his aunt looked afraid, then hatred and desire to air revenge that had lain festering for years sprang to the forefront. 'From letters that *her* father,' she glared at Chantal, 'wrote to the Comtesse and which I intercepted. Oh, he was clever, the young lieutenant,' she snapped her fingers with contempt, 'his letters were carefully phrased so that any reference to poverty or self-pity was omitted, but he was not clever enough to hoodwink me! I knew that his basic aim was money, and a home for his children—by destroying his letters I made certain that he received neither!'

CHAPTER THIRTEEN

A HEAVY, sweet smell hung over the whole of the Province. The vintage was in full swing. Since the first basket of grapes had arrived outside the sheds for pressing work had began and was due to continue non-stop, twenty-four hours a day, until the last of the many baskets filled with luscious amethyst grapes had been disgorged into waiting presses.

Chantal had seen little of Brut since the vintage began, a few snatched moments of conversation were all he had allowed her as, wearing overalls and rubber boots, he had worked side by side with men who, bleary-eyed with weariness, had cheerfully abandoned family, leisure and even sleep to become part of a world consisting solely of tons upon tons of grapes.

She had visited the sheds only once, just as huge vats filled with must were beginning the *bouillage*, a phase during which grape skins floated to the top of the pressed juice and formed layers through which gas erupted in a froth that foamed, bubbled and hissed, creating an atmosphere of stormy anger similar to that that had broken over the head of Madame Mortemart seconds after she had confessed her treachery to Brut. The following day she and Nicole had left hurriedly to begin a prolonged visit to relatives in a distant neighbourhood, but for many days afterwards Brut's anger had remained active as the *bouillage* and even yet traces of a still-simmering storm could be detected in eyes that had hardened to a cold, hard blue. It was as if he held himself partly to blame, Chantal told herself, vexed by the inconsistency of his shouldering responsibility for a deed perpetrated when he was no more than a child.

'It is his pride that is hurt, mademoiselle.' Intuitively, Hortense had guessed the cause of her worry. 'As head of his family, he feels his aunt's action as a slight upon his personal honour.'

Chantal had dismissed the surmise with a shrug. However much it hurt to believe it, however much she wanted to *disbelieve* it, the fact remained that honour had no place in the make-up of a man who had schemed successfully to wreck her future.

Standing in the kitchen of Trésor d'Hélène, she stared bleakly out of the window, hating the thought of leaving the house she had come to regard as home, of never again seeing the green, quiet, graceful landscape which, like the man uppermost in her mind, possessed a *douceur*, a sweetness that compelled affection, as well as a tendency towards sudden storms, shocking in their intensity.

Hortense cut short her orgy of misery by rapping the table with a ladle. 'You did say that you would give me a hand with the food for tonight's *cochelet*, did you not? All this extra work,' she grumbled, 'yet instead of helping you stand for hours mooning at the window!'

'I'm sorry, Hortense,' Chantal whipped round to face her, knowing that the old woman's sharp utterances were shielding concern, 'tell me what I can do to help you.'

'You can prepare the vegetables for the *potée champenoise*,' the housekeeper relented with bad grace. Lifting the lid, she peered into the interior of a huge boiler inside which was simmering a mixture of salted breast of pork, stewing beef, sausages, ham, chickens, seasoning and spices which was to form the basis of the *cochelet*, the huge meal traditionally supplied to the vineyard workers when picking was drawing to an end. 'Hand me the large fork,' she instructed Chantal, then began fishing inside the monster casserole for the sausages which she removed, then popped inside the oven to keep warm. 'Will Monsieur le Marquis and yourself be joining in the festivities this evening, mademoiselle?'

'I doubt it, Hortense.' Carefully Chantal continued shredding cabbages, hoping she would take the hint and abandon the subject.

'But you must both put in an appearance at the *cochelet*!' Hortense protested, scandalised. 'A girl will have been chosen to present you with a bouquet of wild flowers and vine leaves and in return the Marquis will be expected to hand round champagne. And you *mustn't* miss the fair! There will be roundabouts, live trout to be fished for and taken away in plastic bags full of water, and many prizes to be won on the sideshows. And yet,' she sighed, 'the *vendange* is not what it used to be. When I was a girl, the arrival of the *vendangeurs* was a great event. They came here in mule carts with wheels so rickety they looked ready to fall off the spindles— nevertheless, children and old people were piled aloft while younger, fitter members of the family followed behind on foot. Not like today,' she sniffed, 'when we are choked with the dust from lorries over-crowded with people and deafened by the noise and whistles of a generation that seemingly cannot exist without commotion. Only one thing remains the same,' she grinned suddenly, 'and that is the number of tummy-aches we are called upon to cure. They never learn,' she shook her head mournfully, 'warnings are always ignored. For the first few days they gorge themselves silly—especially the children. Do you know, mademoiselle, in the old days we were forced to muzzle even the donkeys because they, too, could not resist nibbling the crisp, sweet grapes!'

'I shall be glad when it's all over,' Chantal sighed, pushing a heavy wing of hair back from her hot forehead, 'for your sake, especially. The arrival of the pickers has caused you a great deal of extra work.'

'They deserve a treat,' Hortense replied simply. 'It is not an easy job, picking grapes from dawn till dusk, especially when they have to be handled so carefully—as if they were globes of fragile glass—in case they should become bruised and start fermenting. They work hard and play hard,' she concluded severely, 'and if I were you I would encourage the Marquis to follow their example.'

Once the vegetables had all been diced and laid aside with peeled potatoes to be added to the casserole during the last hour of cooking, Chantal prepared the batter for Hortense's speciality sweet, *tarte de Cambrai*, peeled and sliced pears for decoration, then sprinkled them with lemon juice to prevent discoloration.

'There, that's the finish!' Her sigh betrayed weariness and deep depression. 'If there are no more chores to be done, Hortense, I think I'll go to my room and lie down for an hour.'

Throwing a quick glance outside to where heavily-foliaged trees were casting pools of shade on to a sward of lawn, where flowers, heavy with petals, were nodding in the path of a gentle breeze and the droning of bees flitting from blossom to blossom added depth to a symphony of peace and tranquility, Hortense seemed about to protest but then, surprising a look of dejection on Chantal's face, she changed her mind.

'Do that, *chérie*,' she urged, her face puckering with concern, 'and don't worry about over-sleeping, I will give you a call long before the festivities are due to begin.'

Chantal did not bother to undress but stretched out supine on the top of her bed, turning her head sideways so that the wedding dress draped across a hanger was in full view. Hortense had worked her usual magic upon the gown of stiff, heavy brocade that even in the days of the notoriously extravagant 'Champagne Girls' had been considered costly. Doves outlined in tiny seed-pearls chased one another, cooing and preening, around the hem of the very full skirt; pearl-studded hearts and lovers' knots embroidered upon cloth aged to the colour of buttercream continued the theme of idyllic love and nuptial harmony.

The image blurred and faded, washed out of

sight by a flood of scalding tears. She wept long and silently—painful, aching tears shed on behalf of the home she was about to lose, the friends she was about to leave behind, and because of the separation imminent between herself and Peter, her only living relative. There was no other reason, she told herself firmly, digging clenched fists deep into the flower-sprigged eiderdown, no other single person whose absence she would regret, yet even while she railed, resisted, denied herself so much as a mention of Brut's name she knew deep within that she was lying.

When at last she surfaced from the depths of despair her mind was cleared of pretence, her heart prepared by her ordeal to face the fact that treacherous, cold-blooded, heartless though the Marquis might be, she was painfully, hopelessly, deeply in love with him.

Accepting this truth brought great relief, no longer would she need to search for excuses for flashes of irritability, for silent, introspective moods, for depression that descended like a cloud at the mere mention of Brut's name. But facing the truth also brought the realisation that she had reached the limit of her endurance; things could not continue as they were, therefore the only solution left to her was to put a swift, sharp end to an intolerable situation.

She prepared for the confrontation as if for the most important night of her life, paying particular attention to her hair which, after it was washed and dried, hugged her shapely head like a cap of bronzed satin. Knowing from experience that no amount of make-up could disguise her scattering of freckles, she stroked a line of green shadow across her eyelids, brushed a mist of pink over lips that would not be still, then with a dejected shrug stepped into a dress of flowered chiffon, its swirling skirt and full sleeves supplying the touch of dignity required of the Marquis's future bride, its softly muted shades of pink, lilac and blue lending to her pale, pointed features the delicacy of a slender spring flower. Her hand hovered over a phial of Muguet des Bois perfume, then withdrew. Perfume, meant as an aid to trick the senses, would be wasted during a scene of confrontation, but then, more as an aid to courage than as an attempt to make their parting memorable, she reached out for the phial and sprayed the haunting fragrance generously on to her skin.

When her toilette was finished she sat gazing with unseeing eyes out of the bedroom window, waiting in a state of numbed acceptance for the time to pass. Vague sounds impinged upon her conscience, the lusty, raucous laughter of pickers returning to makeshift quarters in the outbuildings, Peter's footsteps as he raced, two at a time, up the stairs, then the sound of his unmelodious voice issuing from the bathroom where he was scrubbing away the sweat of the day and preparing himself for the evening's festivities.

Hortense's call, when it came, sounded strident as an alarm. 'Time to get dressed, mademoiselle, the meal is ready and waiting to be served. Monsieur le Marquis has already arrived!'

Calmly, because in her frozen state haste was impossible, Chantal stood up and crossed over to her dressing-table to withdraw a bundle of papers from a drawer. Thrusting them deep into her handbag, she snapped the clasp shut, then walked steadily, with head held erect, towards the door.

Trestle tables covered with chequered cloths were ranged around the courtyard. Incredibly, the pickers who less than half an hour earlier had trailed hot, tired and sweaty from the vineyard were already washed, changed and seated, waiting for the meal to be served. Someone began playing a concertina and a couple began to dance. The sound of voices teasing, flirting, arguing rose loudly on the air.

She stiffened, feeling an impulse to flee, when she saw Brut approaching, but as if he had sensed her thought he quickened his step and captured her hand in his to raise it high in acknowledgement of lusty greetings.

'Smile, *ma petite* ...' As he bent to murmur in her ear their watchers gained an impression of intimacy which they evidently found enjoyable. A rousing cheer rang out, followed by a male voice impudently urging, 'Kiss her, Monsieur le Marquis! All women prefer to kiss rather than to talk!'

Chantal blushed a fiery red when the pickers, already well fortified by wine, fell about laughing. Yet even her sweet solemnity was no proof against the wit of a woman who yelled out a denial. Not always, Jacques—whichever woman you might kiss would be wise to count her teeth!'

The ensuing ribaldry set the tenor of the evening. The setting was perfect, balmy air, sunshine adding warmth to the intimacy of the enclosed, flower-filled courtyard, music rising above the sound of happy voices to mingle with the delicious aroma of food being dished out by Hortense and her willing helpers.

'You must try not to mind their rather earthy humour,' Brut murmured as they took their seats at the head of the centre table.

'Of course I don't mind.' She managed a nervous smile, very conscious of the nearness of his plank-lean body. He was dressed in black—the colour of devilment—and beneath the collar of an open-necked shirt a chain glinted gold against his chest, a chain that shifted as he moved, revealing its burden—a tiny, insignificant signet ring.

Panicked by the unexpected sight, she grabbed the object nearest to her, a pepperpot, and began feverishly sprinkling its contents over the bowl of thin soup that had been placed before her. Sensing his questioning stare, she burst into a babble of embarrassed conversation.

'It's easy to guess that these people are strangers to the neighbourhood—their looks, speech, even their attitude to life is noticeably different from that of the locals.'

'Which is hardly surprising, considering their vastly different backgrounds,' he defended. 'Approximately ten thousand people come here each year to pick the grapes, the hard core of the influx consisting mainly of miners and industrial workers who are encouraged by their own local inspectors of health to spend their holidays in the clean, pure air of the vineyards. Others can be classed as agricultural vagabonds, forever on the move, following the direction of whichever crops are ready for harvest-

ing. The rest is made up of gypsies, students, and
the unemployed.'

Chantal pretended to concentrate on her soup, yet
was unaware of its peppery bite upon her tongue.
'They must enjoy coming here if they arrive regularly, year after year,' she mumbled, thrashing the
utmost out of the conversation.

'For most of them this is the only type of holiday
they can afford, for others it is a case of carrying
out a family tradition, but all of them, whether they
come from habit, for money, or,' he twinkled, 'as
in the case of the younger element, for sex, they
all make certain that on this night especially they
thoroughly enjoy themselves.'

Once more, hot colour was goaded into her cheeks
by his deliberately wicked reference. Deciding that
such earthiness was best left ignored, she pushed
aside her plate and looked around the table, anxious
to lose herself in the anonymity of casual conversation. But every man present seemed to have but one
objective in mind; each had an arm hooked around
the waist of a girl-friend, leaving the other hand
free to ply fork or spoon; each was busy whispering
words so amusing most of the girls had collapsed
into helpless giggles, each was intent upon ensuring
that glasses were kept filled to the brim with *vin
diable,* the devil's wine.

'Drink up,' Brut urged lazily, topping up her half-
filled glass.

A surge of anger brought about by the gullibility
of her own sex found relief in a scornful refusal. 'No,
thank you! Looking around, it appears to me that
"drink in, wits out" is a maxim that has the full
approval of your male associates!' Bravely she chal-

lenged his amused glance with eyes of bright, courageous green. 'Sorry to disappoint you, but your traditional sport doesn't appeal to me—I have no intention of accepting a bottle of bubbly in exchange for a toss in the hay!'

To her fury, instead of being deflated Brut threw back his head and roared with laughter. She wanted to jump up and run, but protocol demanded that she should remain; in the eyes of the *vendangeurs* the Marquis was the *grand seigneur*, it was unthinkable that his betrothed should not be proud and happy to wait his pleasure.

Suddenly, with a softness more startling than a shout, he bent close to admonish, 'Don't tempt fate, *ma petite*, we Champenois hold a belief that has seldom been proved wrong—it is that the harvest will be ready to be gathered ninety days after the first lilies have flowered. *Today is the ninetieth day!*'

He had no need to elaborate, to spell out that his reference to the reaping of the harvest had nothing whatsoever to do with the gathering of grapes. For ten long, weary days and nights the men labouring in the vineyard had been in no mood to embrace anything other than celibacy, but now, as stripped of weariness as the vines were stripped of grapes, they were ready and willing to seek intoxication either from a bottle or from a woman's lips—but preferably from both!

It was almost midnight by the time Chantal decided that she had stood as much as she could take of the man in whose restless shadow she felt trapped. Not once had he left her side. For the whole of the evening as riotous gaiety washed around them, she had been made very aware of his intimidating presence, had felt like a mouse being stalked by a tiger, her every stride outmatched, her every evasive tactic thwarted. She was dancing woodenly in his arms, fighting against an urge to match the hypnotic rhythm of his body as he held her against him, communicating with a light touch of fingers along her spine an urgent plea to relax, to become soft and pliable.

Sensing his eyes lazily assessing her reaction, she stumbled, then jerked out of reach before his arms could tighten.

'I don't want to dance any more,' she gasped, 'I'm tired. But before I go to my room there's something we must discuss.' Wildly she looked around, seeking escape from the mill of noisy pickers who were becoming more boisterous by the minute. Shrieks of laughter coming from inside the house made plain the uselessness of seeking solitude there, so, taking her by the hand, Brut guided her out of the well-lighted courtyard in the direction of the dark, deserted vineyard. Furtive movements and half-stifled giggles betrayed the presence of other couples taking advantage of night's dark blanket, but these sounds gradually died out until, by the time they stopped to lean against a gate, a dull throbbing pulse of silence lay all around them.

'Well, Chantal?' He sounded grave. 'Are you ready to tell me whatever it is that is troubling you?'

Surprised by the absence of the devilment that had teased her nerves all evening, she fumbled open her bag, withdrew a bundle of papers, and thrust them into his hand. 'I want to give you these. And this ...' As an afterthought, she began tugging the huge emerald ring from her finger, but before she had eased it over her knuckle her hand was enclosed within a steely grip.

'Leave it!' he rapped.

'No, I will not!' She almost sobbed in her frustration. 'I'm sick of lies and deceit, I want to go home to England,' to her horror her voice developed a wobble, 'I've given you everything you want, so there's no further need for pretence.'

'What have you given me, Chantal?' He sounded calm, yet the grip of his fingers was intense.

'I've given you the deeds to Trésor d'Hélène,' she choked, feeling suddenly weary. 'Please don't try to deny that your proposal was a deliberate ploy to gain possession of the vineyard. I overheard Nicole and her mother talking, you see,' she sounded almost sorry for him, 'perhaps it was wrong of me to eavesdrop, but I'm glad I did, for at least I was left with no illusions about your sincerity while you were acting out the part of a man in love.'

'So ...' The hissed exclamation sounded agonised. 'At last I have discovered the reason behind the existence of your hard shell which I always suspected was donned especially for me! You thought me a liar, yet you never allowed me to guess how revolted you were by my kisses, how you inwardly shuddered from my touch, how cynically unmoved you were by my amorous declarations!' Fear grabbed her by the throat, fear of the man whose utter stillness projected deep and terrible anger. 'Did it never occur to you, Chantal,' the steel thread of his voice continued, 'that you might have been mistaken? Was there no secret part of you that refused to believe me capable of such treachery, do you possess none of the feminine intuition which supposedly is invaluable in helping to distinguish a sincere man from a rogue?'

Casting control to the winds, he shocked her by grating, 'Never before have I pandered so long to the whims of one woman, never has my patience been so stretched, my emotions kept so rigidly under control, and all on account of a freckle-faced, tormenting, tantalising witch who dangled me at arm's length for her own secret amusement!' All the built-up frustration of previous weeks was present in the force with which he jerked her hard against his body. 'If a man is punished before he has sinned,' he threatened thickly, 'how can he be blamed for claiming the enjoyment he has already paid for?'

He had kissed her before, but never with such brutal intensity; he had touched and caressed her, but never had she been made to feel as if fingers of fire were branding marks of possession upon her flesh. Desire raged rampant through the whip-lean body of the man who used her as a desert nomad would use a crystal pool to slake his thirst, as a deprived drunkard, driven to excess, would drain a bottle to its dregs.

White-hot fear gripped her, yet incredibly it was fear born not of his demented kisses, of the hoarse, strained voice of a man nearing the edge of control, but fear that had jumped into glorious life with the realisation that she might possibly have misjudged him. Too buffeted by emotion to think straight, too stifled by his kisses to ask the questions raging to be answered, she clung to him and felt her shy innocence overcome by a surge of violent feeling that impelled heated response into lips that had offered stiff, cool resistance to his onslaught. Simultaneously, her hands crept up behind his neck and fingers with a will of their own began running riot through his hair.

The effect of her surrender was startling. Pressed as close as one, his great, heaving shudder racked them both. Then he fell still, the muscles beneath her hands tensing hard as rock. The shock when he stepped backward, putting a yard of space between them, was so great that she could only stand and stare, her eyes wide with hurt puzzlement. She heard a breath rasp harshly in his throat, sensed the tremendous effort he made to sound controlled when he apologised:

'I'm sorry, Chantal. It must seem to you that you are fated always to suffer at the hands of myself and other members of my family. Already we have robbed you of the love and companionship of a wonderful old lady, your grandmother. Through us, you were denied the upbringing that was your right and the inheritance which reluctantly the broken-hearted old Comtesse willed to others. Then, as if that was not enough,' he grated, 'I, too, for a few insane moments was determined to rob you. Thank God, I managed to find strength enough to resist inflicting the ultimate atrocity.'

She wanted to run across the yawning space dividing them, to caress his ravaged face, to kiss the sternness from his mouth, to whisper assurances that would chase the bleak look of despair from his eyes. But her limbs refused to respond. Like a statue frozen to immobility, she could communicate only through stricken eyes.

That her message had been misread was evident when the proud Marquis began to plead, 'Try to forgive me, Chantal—not yet, it is too soon—but some day please try to believe that I have never lied, that everything I have done I did with your interests at heart. How could it be otherwise when I love you so, Chantal, a love that began for me on the day that you opened your door and found me standing on your doorstep.'

The admission almost broke her heart. With a sob of compassion she flew to him, then, hugging him tightly around the waist, her head buried deep in his chest, she began to sob.

'Brut! Brut, my darling, I love you ... I love you!'

For one nerve-racking moment he remained rigid, then with a sigh of incredulous relief he gathered her close and laying his cheek against her hair began to rock her tenderly.

It was not a moment for speech, their hearts were too full, their emotions too ravaged for words. Passion, joy, jubilation were all to come, but at that moment all they wanted was to cling together, bemused with wonder, appalled by the realisation of how near they had come to disaster.

'*Amour de mon cœur,*' finally he managed a broken whisper, 'welcome home, my own, my adorable Champagne girl!'

Choose from this list of Harlequin Romance editions.

Relive a great love story...
Harlequin Romances 1980
Complete and mail this coupon today!

Harlequin Reader Service

In U.S.A.
MPO Box 707
Niagara Falls, N.Y. 14302

In Canada
649 Ontario St.
Stratford, Ontario, N5A 6W2

Please send me the following Harlequin Romance novels. I am enclosing my check or money order for $1.25 for each novel ordered, plus 59¢ to cover postage and handling.

☐ 449	☐ 528	☐ 658	☐ 804	☐ 904	☐ 451
☐ 454	☐ 532	☐ 711	☐ 805	☐ 911	☐ 462
☐ 464	☐ 538	☐ 712	☐ 856	☐ 918	☐ 468
☐ 469	☐ 557	☐ 730	☐ 861	☐ 409	☐ 478
☐ 494	☐ 597	☐ 766	☐ 890	☐ 430	☐ 485
☐ 500	☐ 604	☐ 796	☐ 892	☐ 438	☐ 489
☐ 513	☐ 627	☐ 800	☐ 895	☐ 443	☐ 491
☐ 516	☐ 643	☐ 802	☐ 901	☐ 446	☐ 495

Number of novels checked @ $1.25 each = $ _____

N.Y. State residents add appropriate sales tax $ _____

Postage and handling $ _____ .59

TOTAL $ _____

I enclose _____
(Please send check or money order. We cannot be responsible for cash sent through the mail.)

Prices subject to change without notice.

NAME _____
(Please Print)

ADDRESS _____

CITY _____

STATE/PROV. _____

ZIP/POSTAL CODE _____

Offer expires September 30, 1980.   0055633

And there's still *more* love in

Yes!

Six more spellbinding
romantic stories every month
by your favorite authors.
Elegant and sophisticated tales of
love and love's conflicts.

Let your imagination be swept away to
exotic places in search of adventure,
intrigue and romance. Get to
know the warm, true-to-life
characters. Share the special
kind of miracle that
love can be.

Don't miss out. Buy now and discover
the world of HARLEQUIN PRESENTS...